THE KISS OF KIN

Also available in
SCRIBNER SIGNATURE EDITIONS

GROWING UP RICH *by Anne Bernays*
SOUTH STREET *by David Bradley*
WHAT I KNOW SO FAR *by Gordon Lish*
DEAR MR. CAPOTE *by Gordon Lish*
VOICES AGAINST TYRANNY *edited by John Miller*
COOL HAND LUKE *by Donn Pearce*
BLOOD TIE *by Mary Lee Settle*
THE LOVE EATERS *by Mary Lee Settle*
20 UNDER 30 *edited by Debra Spark*
STATE OF GRACE *by Joy Williams*

THE KISS OF KIN

Mary Lee Settle

SCRIBNER**SIGNATURE**EDITION

CHARLES SCRIBNER'S SONS • NEW YORK
1986

This novel is a work of fiction. Names, characters, places and incidents are either the product of the author's imagination or are used fictitiously. Any resemblance to actual persons, living or dead, events or locales is entirely coincidental.

Library of Congress Cataloging-in-Publication Data

Settle, Mary Lee.
The kiss of kin.
Reprint. Originally published: 1955.
I. Title.
PS3569.E84K57   1986   813'.54   86-11874
ISBN 0-684-18715-9

Copyright 1955 by Mary Lee Settle;
copyright renewed ©1983 by Mary Lee Settle
All rights reserved
Published simultaneously in Canada by Collier Macmillan Canada, Inc.

Originally published in hardcover by Harper & Row

First Signature Edition 1986

Printed in the United States of America.

Cover art "Ornamental Love" by Robert Longo.
Courtesy of the artist and Metro Pictures, New York.
Private collection, London.

TO MY MOTHER AND FATHER WITH MY LOVE AND THANKS FOR ALL THEIR HELP WHILE I WAS WRITING THIS BOOK

CHAPTER I

JESUS IS COMING—ARE YOU READY?
When you've seen this sign, whitewashed high on the blasted cliff-face above the hairpin curve of the mountain pass, you will know you've reached the Holy Roller country. The bare rocks are so high and jut sometimes so far over the deep-cut gorges that you find yourself imagining, as you swing around the sickening but well-graded highway, that the people who care about catching you in such mountain danger to both your soul and your body have flown up like birds in their astounding faith to paint the warnings.

Abraham Passmore, driving over the mountain westward, missed the warning sign which flashed above his line of vision as he took the curve at a careful, controlled sixty. By the time he came down to the bridge over the Canona river, and had left the gorge behind for the flat river road, the afternoon sun was full in his face, so that he missed the turning and had to go five miles back up the river again.

After the cool of the mountain pass, the creek road was hazy with summer dust, which tanned the bare boards of the store porches and deadened the bright advertising posters nailed to the shed walls. The houses of the scratch farms looked blanketed and asleep. Abraham saw a few men in overalls perched on unpainted railings, staring at the road, completely still. All the way up Clear Creek to the house of his grandmother, he saw no movement, even among the animals. It was too hot.

By the time he reached the house, the chromium clock on the dash-board read a quarter past three, so he pulled his Buick into the weeds of the roadside and settled back to watch the shut doors.

His first impression was bitter disillusion. The clapboard house, set sideways of the creek, needed a coat of paint. The yard on the creek-side was full of crab-grass and bare brown patches. Although in the front some attempt at a broad lawn had been made, it lay sun-browned and tired-looking between the front porch and the branch. The far side of the house had been built so near the hill behind it that it seemed to grow from the steep slope itself and still lean on it for support. The front door, shut against the heat, had hung on it a large wreath, curled and dead from having been in the sun in the morning, but now drooping in the afternoon shadow of the porch. Down beside the deserted path to the front gate straggled dusty tiger-lilies.

The long kitchen ell, with its high porch all around it, was awash in the sun, but even under the pall of heat the back room of the main house had its windows tight shut. In the front room, Abraham could see that the dark blinds were drawn; little winds puffed and sucked them in and out of the open windows. Down behind the house, along the side-road, there were five or six cars, he couldn't see how many, only that there was no room for him to park. The whole stillness of it, even the stillness of a small girl in the distance, squatting down by the back steps, was like the outside of a church during the service, a breath-holding stillness, hot, suspended.

Abraham leaned back and lit a cigarette; the disappointment at the smallness of what he saw brought his dark face down into an almost childish scowl, which he inspected in his car-mirror, then let the inspection carry over into an examination of his dark chin. But he could not keep his eyes away from the farmhouse for long. He found himself staring at the corner of the yard where the clapboard outhouses and the hog-pen seemed to teeter backwards towards the creek water, top-heavy, awkward, and all of it little from across the creek, too little for Abraham Passmore's peace of mind. He sighed and said, "Oh Jesus!" and began to comb his thick brown hair.

Inside the kitchen, big, spare-boned A'nt Elemere stood stirring the green-beans and trying, when she could remember through her own numbness, to keep the children quiet. She stood in the shadow of the coal-range, where the three-o'clock sun, stretching through the side-yard screen-door and the big screened windows, could not reach her. In a circle above the huge, empty kitchen table drowsy flies hung in the air.

John Junior, eight years old, yawned widely and let his mouth stay opened to whine.

"It feels jist like Sunday." He watched A'nt Elemere's board-straight back, and then concentrated on her black right ear to see if he could make her turn round and pay some attention to him. He began to kick the low cabinet under one of the windows where he sat with his feet dangling heavily over the edge. She still didn't pay any attention even when he increased it to a heavy drumming. The sun threw his shadow across the floor, made a halo of his tow-head, caught the rims of his glasses as he turned towards A'nt Elemere, complaining because even the kicking had failed.

"I haven't got anything to do!"

"Shhh . . . up." A'nt Elemere was miles away from him, but he had at last managed to drag her back for a second to her duty.

"Why don' you jist shut up?" she asked him, over her shoulder.

"When are we gonna eat dinner?"

"You had a big samich."

"A samich is nothin'," John Junior muttered, and looked around the room again for something to do. This time he noticed the wall telephone and jumped down from the cabinet.

"I'm gonna call up somebody." He said it tentatively, expecting her to say 'no, not to,' but she only tasted the beans.

"Reach me the salt."

He handed it to her, running across the room from the kitchen cabinet. When she took it from his hand, she did it slowly, without even looking, just groping for it, so obviously far away where her eyes were staring, that John Junior was awed for a second, but he soon got over that, and said, almost whispering, so he could swear he told her, "I think I'll call up Digby."

He stretched up to the wall telephone, pulled its mouth down with his lips almost inside it, and pushed the receiver hard against his ear. Then he carefully put his elbow up on the lever, holding it down to ring, winding, three times softly.

When he got his answer and spoke, his voice smacked wet and urgent against the black mouth; he remembered to whisper, so that what he said sounded frighteningly important. "Hello, Digby, this is John. I can't come out today. My grandmaw's dead." He obviously wasn't satisfied with the comment he got. "I'm not bragging, I just thought I'd tell you again."

A'nt Elemere heard him and interrupted softly. "Passed over, honey, passed over."

"She had a stroke. I don't know what it is. Well, just a stroke, that's all. Well my grandmaw did die of hers even if your grandmaw didn't die of hers. I don't know whether she went all stiff or not. Nobody wouldn't let me see. Do you want to go down to the creek tomorrow?" The answer made him defend himself hotly and conventionally, "You have not! You've only got to stay in on the day if they die! They're having the funeral right now in the dining-room. It is not funny. Grandmaw's coffin is too big and expensive to get it out the living-room door. I heard A'nt Amelia . . ."

A'nt Elemere rushed furiously and grabbed the telephone receiver, slamming it down on the hook.

"Gimme that phone! You jest shut up that there kind of talk!" She was almost crying, so her voice made John Junior apologise, quietly, "I didn't say nothin'."

She coached him by habit, as she had heard the white women do a thousand times.

"Innything."

"Honest, I didn't do innything. Stop fussing at me." But she had already stopped caring. She sank down at the big kitchen table, and he realised she wasn't going to fuss, or even see him on such a day.

He wandered away from her then and leaned gazing out of the side-yard screen-door at Mary Armstrong, who was playing at the porch steps. He couldn't see what it was she had in her hand; she had a secretive way of playing. All he could see was her back as she squatted daintily, prissily, on pointed feet in the grass.

Abraham, seeing a shadow in the doorway, thought it was the funeral over and stubbed his cigarette, wondering just how he'd start it, how to break in. But when no one appeared but a little boy he settled back again to wait, staring down the road, coldly.

John Junior, watching Mary Armstrong with her eyes half-lidded, already sneaking up a secret in his mind, interrupted her.

"Whatcha doing, Mary Armstrong?"

She didn't turn round, but she remembered to speak in a loud whisper. "Nothin'," she said. "Get away." Her talk was as prissy as her feet. She spoke carefully, as if more people than little old John Junior might be listening.

"Can I play?"

"No. You're too dirty. You say too many dirty words and I can smell your socks when you get too close to me." She smoothed her own smocked dimity, and went on to scratch her bottom.

"You can not!" John Junior was elaborately casual. "Anyway I don't want to play innything."

But his curiosity was overwhelming because he was bored.

"What's that?" He didn't bother to open the screen-door, just pressed his face against it, craning to see what she had in her hand.

"None of your beeswax," she closed her fist.

"Any other day you'd be itching to play with me."

"Well, I'm not today," said Mary Armstrong, conscious of a power of choice she didn't often feel.

"Come on in here!"

"I can't." She bent down almost double to put whatever it was under the step. "Mama told me if she caught me inside the house today she'd tan my hide."

"Can you see innything from there?" John Junior rolled his face sideways against the screen and tried to look down the long porch.

Mary Armstrong straightened up and took on a grown-up, solemn air as she tiptoed to see through the dining-room window.

"A little bit," she whispered. "Isn't it terrible, though?"

Then she was too interested to remember that the occasion was a solemn one; she stretched and stared.

"Mama's crying into her handkerchief. Ole A'nt Mary

The Kiss of Kin

Lee's looking all stiff. A'nt Cinnybug's acting like crying but she's really peeking through her hands at Mary Margaret. I'll betcha she's trying to remember her top so's she can make one like it. There's little old Sary Jane. She got to go and she's as young as me. It isn't fair."

Mary Armstrong laughed with a 'heee' and covered her mouth.

"Sary Jane's picking her nose like anything. My mama says it's trashy for youngins to go to funerals."

But John Junior had already grown bored with what he hadn't spirit enough in the heat to open the door and see for himself.

"Do you want to know a secret?"

"No." She was impatient with him, intent on the funeral as she was, using him only to tell it all to.

"Cousin Cad's crying."

"He would."

"That Julik looks bored."

"Oh well, he don't know innything. He's not even Amer'can."

Their voices, forgetting, growing stronger, reached through A'nt Elemere's sorrow for a minute. She roused herself to call.

"John Junior, come on in here!"

He ignored her, because at last he had Mary Armstrong nibbling with interest in him, like a little fish.

"Don't you want to know what the secret is?"

"What?"

She came to the screen-door, smoothing her dress against her stomach all unawares, although she'd been caught so often before.

He whispered, a wet hiss through the screen. What he whispered caused Mary Armstrong's face to open, then to pucker up. She began to yell.

John Junior having finally succeeded in luring her there could think of little nasty enough to punish Mary Armstrong for having ignored him for so long. But, having a natural talent for obscenity, he managed.

"I'm gonna tell my mama on you!" She went on howling.

A'nt Elemere jumped into action. She flung John Junior out of the way, pushed open the screen-door and grabbed Mary Armstrong.

"Mary Armstrong, shut up. I'll jist naturally maim you if you hollar like that agin."

The dining-room door opened slowly; a sanctimonious voice could be heard for a minute, reciting in a silent room: "For this corruptible must put on incorruption, and this mortal must put on immortality . . ."

The voice was shut out as the door was closed again, and Amelia Passmore Edwards, Mary Armstrong's mother, tiptoed into the room, looking just about worn out. She was in green-black mourning, a kind of drab fancy-dress, got together from odds and ends for the day. Her plump, white face showed all the signs of silent, handkerchief-gagged crying. She was twisting the damp knot of her handkerchief in her hands as she leaned against the door, to feel it close behind her softly.

"For heaven's sake, A'nt Elemere, can't you keep these youngins quiet? You can hear them all the way in there!" in a gentle plaintive voice, but when she turned to find Mary Armstrong the slight whine was gone. She sounded as though she meant business. "Mary Armstrong, I thought I told you to keep away from that door!"

Amelia looked round the door for her, her whole body poised to go on fussing; but there was only John Junior, standing caught in the sun. She sank back into the shadows and heaved a big sigh. Mary Armstrong at the first sound of her mother had run tiptoe, and her path was marked by a squawking runcus as she dodged through the chicken yard.

"I'm sorry, Miss Amelia, I don't reckon I was payin' 'em enough attention," A'nt Elemere told her, looking at John Junior. Her whisper was light to match Amelia's, then she called, stridently but quietly, to John Junior. "Now git on outside, John Junior, and if I hear one sound out of you I'll jest naturally pull you apart."

John Junior moseyed out of the screen-door, letting it bang with a quiver behind him. Amelia didn't see him go. She was too intent on bending down to the low cabinet to pick out a shot-glass, and carrying it carefully to the kitchen cabinet. She poured the last of a drink out of a bottle of corn whisky, balanced the drink in one hand, crossed the room and threw the bottle neatly into the garbage can under the drain-board. Then she seemed to wilt down to the table, carefully resting the shot-glass on it as if she were doing some secret balancing trick.

"I can't go back in there without a little something to buck me up," she muttered, more to herself than to A'nt Elemere, as she took off her black hat, fluffed her marcelled, once blonde hair up from where it had lain damp against her sad face. A'nt Elemere went and stood so near that she could feel the heat from her big body, a hotter shadow than the sun had been on her back.

"Miss Amelia, I wouldn't do that today if I was you." She spoke so that the boy wouldn't hear, touching her shoulder to get her attention.

But Amelia only waved her out of the light, then turned to squint up at her, still waving monotonously, shooing her, saying, "Let me alone," and again, more strongly,

"A'nt Elemere, let me alone!" She picked up the glass with her little finger crooked tea-party and delicate, paused, then knocked the drink back.

When A'nt Elemere didn't answer she went on, complaining, "It's none of your business. You make too much around here your business lately."

"All right, Miss Amelia." A'nt Elemere shrugged and turned away, giving up, too numb to care anyway. "Don't git riled at me," she said by habit; then she spied John Junior leaning on the screen-door again, and took it out on him.

"Quit hangin' around that door. I thought I told you to run on out there and let me alone."

John Junior paid her no mind. He sidled into the kitchen.

"I forgot something." He came close to Amelia.

"What you drinkin', A'nt Amelia?"

"Nothin'. Just a little tonic."

"Can I have a taste?"

"No. John Junior, go on outside!" Amelia begged him wearily, and turned her face away by habit so that he couldn't smell her breath.

"I haven't got innything to do," he hummed by habit, almost leaning against her.

She edged away from him. "Well, go and find something."

A'nt Elemere interrupted, worried, "Don't you think you better go on back in there?"

Amelia's head sank into her hand, propped up by her elbow on the table, spread-eagled. She touched the shot-glass again, turning it.

"I can't go back in there. I'd be sick." Her voice was so low that A'nt Elemere had to move nearer and nearer to hear the weary whispered complaining. "They've shut the windows so's to keep the flies out while the service is going on, and the smell of all those store-bought flowers makes me sick. Oh Lord, what a day...." Her head was sinking nearer the oil-cloth table-top as if it were too heavy to hold up any more.

John Junior settled down across the table to stare at her. All of the grown-ups had been avoiding him all day and he was fascinated by this withdrawal into sadness which seemed to shut him out.

"That's your mother in there, isn't it?"

"What a funny thing to say, son! You know very well it's Mother." Amelia's head went erect with surprise at his odd question, and she sounded pathetic suddenly, saying 'mother' for a woman so newly dead, knowing he had heard her shriek another name at the old woman as she lolled crazily drunk over the stair-well quarrelling with her not one month ago.

"Now you know that, honey," she said again, finding death embarrassing in front of the child.

"Did granmaw hit you when you were a little girl?" John Junior was so curious his bottom twitched.

"Don't talk like that," Amelia told him, sternly, "it isn't nice."

"Why not?"

"Well, she's dead, son." All at once she just couldn't be bothered. "Now go on out and let me alone."

John Junior started to go. He began at least to unwind from his chair, but slowly; he was not satisfied.

"Well, did she?"

"Yes. Sometimes. But she was worried. We all got on her nerves." He had made her remember, and she sounded for a minute as prissy as Mary Armstrong. "She used to take after us, with a stick."

Amelia closed her memory then like a book, and added

because she thought she ought, "But she was a mighty fine woman, don't you ever forget it."

"In this kitchen?" John Junior was too fascinated to be put off.

"Sometimes in this kitchen."

"Like you do Mary Armstrong?"

Amelia swept her hand out towards him, half shooing, half hitting at the air, angry, "Go on out and play, John Junior, before I take you in hand!"

John Junior moved just out of the range of her arm.

"I haven't got innything to do."

Amelia forgot and almost shouted at him, "Git on out of here!"

Before he could move A'nt Elemere had bunched him up in one arm and, holding open the door with her foot, shoved him like a bundle of dirty laundry out on to the porch. He ran down the steps, and stopped, remembering that Mary Armstrong had hidden something under them. He squatted down. It was only a pebble. He shoved it into his pocket and ran off down the side-yard.

The dining-room door opened again and Amelia was warned of someone coming by the minister's voice, now intoning on his sad notes:

"Deal graciously, we pray thee, with those who mourn, that casting every care . . ."

The door shut out the minister's voice.

When Amelia saw that it was Mary Lee, she twisted the shot-glass quickly into her damp handkerchief and cupped the whole into her closed fist. Mary Lee, her lips like a dry slit, and her temples banging so that Amelia could see them throb, had not slipped over yet into fury; the whole situation was too formal for fury. As she looked at Amelia, sloppy in the heat, her back straightened like a ramrod.

"Well, I think at least you might drag yourself back to

come to the grave." Grey-haired Mary Lee had developed a voice as biting and cold as the chop of an axe. She used it now, full force, on the blonde, fat woman slumped against the table. "What are people to think with you running out in the middle of the ceremony?"

She had to stop looking at Amelia, and it weakened her disapproval, but she could see the criss-cross pattern of the oil-cloth table-cover when she did, and the lines trembled and became alive at the corner of her eyes, which were already seeing flat visions in the still time before the storm of a migraine. She tried to bring her mind back to her duty, getting Amelia up out of the chair.

But Amelia was too tired even to be bullied. She only muttered, "A funeral isn't a ceremony. It's a service," as she stuffed the handkerchief into the pocket of her short jacket. Mary Lee didn't bother to notice the gesture.

"Don't think ever' last one of them didn't know exactly what for!" she told Amelia, to make sure she didn't think she could ever fool a soul.

Like a magician keeping up the trick sadly after he has lost his audience, Amelia took the now empty handkerchief out and wiped her forehead and begged the skinny judge who stood over her, keeping the sun away: "Oh, Mary Lee, don't keep harping on things today of all days. Can't you see I'm upset?"

"Don't you think I'm upset, too?" Mary Lee was impatient. "I nearly cried right in the middle of the service. Come on and don't give in to yourself so much."

This time she took hold of Amelia's arm and piloted her back into the dining-room. After she had let go, and settled down among the others to pray in the hot, airless room, the marks of her fingers stayed through the rest of the funeral on Amelia's soft, white arm.

CHAPTER II

"A'NT ELEMERE! A'nt Elemere!" John Junior ran to the screen-door, calling in a breathy squeak which was the nearest he could come to a whisper. He was far too excited at the thought of the parade to remember that it was a death march, for he went on, big-eyed, urging her to the screen-door by flapping his hand at her. "Come on quick. They're fixin' to carry it out."

A'nt Elemere hurried across the kitchen to where a small, three-cornered piece of mirror hung on a string, half hidden behind the kitchen cabinet. She stood in front of it, adjusting her high black felt hat, the tears streaming at last, without any damming sobs, down her black face. Then she took her stand, solemnly adjusting her skirt, inside the screen-door out of the way, to watch the procession pass.

John Junior lingered just outside. "Why didn't you go in there to the funeral?" he asked her, having asked the question already several times, but hoping in the new excitement finally to get an answer.

A'nt Elemere opened the door and pulled him in to stand beside her.

"Because the Southern Episcopal Church ain't suitin' to me or Miss Anna Mary," she told him. "All them books, and them writ-down prayers. Standin' up. Settin' down . . ." Her voice died away as she saw a black-suited man opening the dining-room door on to the porch.

The Reverend Beedie Jenkins eased himself in through the back screen-door just as the first of the procession carrying the coffin started out through the dining-room door and down the side porch through the sun. He was a tall, raw-boned white man, his face burned Indian colour by farming in the hot sun. He had on a black suit too, but it was shiny at the elbows, with the sleeves coming to just above his long, skinny wrists. If his suit was too little for his body, his eyes seemed too big for his gaunt head. They lay deep in their sockets, snap-black, the livest thing about the man.

"Sister Elemere," he whispered, but came in at the same time and stood beside her.

"They're jest bringin' 'er out." A'nt Elemere's hand went up to brush away a fly, and came away from her face wet with tears.

A few men with pale office faces, and dressed in sober winter black, came by the screen-door silently, looking behind them crabwise, as if in front, they knew they ought to be behind the coffin.

Brother Beedie looked down at the floor getting ready to pray, but mumbling first.

"Sister Elemere, we ought to of beried 'er."

He spoke slowly, deep into his chest like a mountaineer.

A'nt Elemere began to nod her head.

"Brother Beedie, this ain't right. It jest ain't nothin' like Miss Anna Mary would of liked." She kept on nodding, forgetting why.

"Yep," he went on, "we ought to of beried Sister Anna Mary. She was ourn and we ought to of done the job."

"It ain't right," A'nt Elemere whispered.

"He works in mysterious ways," said Brother Beedie. "If she'd of lived longer, she'd of constructed a tabernacle of truth like she always said she would. We woulda done it from thar—right."

"She meant to, Brother Beedie, she meant to."

"I knowed she meant to."

The Kiss of Kin

The heavy black casket, shaped like a Georgian serving dish with tasteful heavy bronze handles, its pall-bearers straining at the weight, started past the door.

"I didn't mean it wudn't on her mind. I knowed that," he said.

None of the pall-bearers had yet begun to match their paces, so they shuffled heavily as if they were moving furniture. The pink waxy rosebuds on the living pall, given by all Miss Anna Mary's children, bobbed like little bells.

A'nt Elemere began to sob.

Reverend Jenkins whispered. "We will kneel here in prayer. There ain't nothin' else we can do."

A'nt Elemere knelt down, her head resting against the screen-door. Mary Lee, passing the door, saw her there, and she whispered to a pale, dark-haired, sad girl who was walking beside her, pushing her out of place in the procession. A'nt Elemere began to pray.

"O holy and humble Jesus of the many mercies, look down on Sister Anna . . ."

The girl slipped through the door and bent low over them.

"A'nt Elemere, youall get up from there. Mother'll just naturally wring your neck. Come on, now."

A'nt Elemere heaved herself up to her feet, crying. Mary Margaret Rosen, Mary Lee's daughter, having done exactly as she was told, sat down exhausted at the table making no move to rejoin the procession, which had by now become orderly, as it filed past the screen-door. Men and women stared into the kitchen as they passed, some very old, some bent, all but ten-year-old Sary Jane, holding her grandmaw's hand, dressed in her Sunday School dress and clutching an old beaded bag. She didn't dare look in like the rest for fear of catching John Junior's eye and giggling, not wanting to . . . it just happening . . .

Mary Margaret turned in her chair to A'nt Elemere, not noticing her anger because her face was so still.

"Is there a cup of coffee for Mr. Rosen?" she asked, "I know he'll feel awful after that service." She turned away again, taking off her black straw hat and ruffing up her dark bangs just as Amelia had done.

Brother Beedie opened the porch door, and asked before stepping out, "Ain't you followin', Sister Elemere?"

A'nt Elemere looked beyond him to where the casket was just being turned, awkwardly, through the back gate.

"No, sir, I done changed my mind," she told him and turned her back on all of them.

Brother Beedie slipped out of the screen-door and joined on at the end of the procession, bowing his head and clutching his hat to his stomach. A'nt Elemere couldn't help but watch for a minute, and then, knowing that Mary Margaret only did what her mother told her to like the rest of them, decided to forget her interrupted prayers and pour some coffee.

"Ain't you goin' up to the vault, Miss Mary Margaret?"

Mary Margaret from behind her sounded far away with fatigue. "No," she said, "I ought to, but to tell you the truth I'm too tired to face the climb. How they can do it . . . Anyway Mr. Rosen's not too well."

"Now ain't that jest too bad?" Ant Elemere began to mutter.

"Aren't you going up?"

The question made A'nt Elemere remember that she still had her hat on. She went across the room, back to the slip of mirror in its private place, took off her hat slowly, inspected it, and hung it up again, then went back and handed Mary Margaret her coffee, looking at the girl closely. With her wide black skirt and her neat black shirt, Mary Margaret managed without knowing it to bring another world, a world of cut hair and ballet slippers, into the kitchen. But that wasn't what was bothering A'nt Elemere. What it was she wasn't saying. Instead she kept on muttering in a voice so low that Julik Rosen, pale as a ghost, neither heard nor saw her when he staggered in from the dining-room.

"That was the hottest hour I've ever had to spend. Christ!" He sat down in a chair where a corner of the table cut into the shade, his thin face white enough to move anyone but A'nt Elemere, who was glaring at him from behind both their backs.

"Drink this, honey." Mary Margaret gave him the coffee. A'nt Elemere silently poured another cup and set it in front of her.

"What a day! Christ, what a business it all is, Mary!" Julik's hand waved to and fro, in and out of the sunlight.

"Mary Margaret," A'nt Elemere began to mutter the name to herself, hating Julik because he'd shortened it so that it sounded just plain Yankee, and used the Lord's name in vain twice in the few minutes he'd been in the room.

Julik heard her then. He seemed to forget the heat for a minute, fascinated by her, obviously wanting to be friendly.

"Why weren't you in the dining-room, Mrs. Freeman? Is it because you are a negro?" He tried to put his sympathy into words, to show her what side he was on. "I think it's pretty bad when they don't let a woman who's served them always come to a funeral."

A'nt Elemere was bored with him before he began. She stared through him, not seeing him for the sun-glare between them. She said, "Oh, don't talk foolishness, Mr. Rosen. I jest didn't want to. That's all."

"The reasons would interest me." He was ready to defend her.

"Would they?"

"I've heard of this kind of business, plenty. But well, you see, I never seen a place like it before. My family..."

A'nt Elemere cut him off with a loud, "Un-hunh!" sullen and abrupt.

Mary Margaret felt unaccountably ashamed of Julik, knowing that he was only trying to be amiable, and that A'nt Elemere was acting like a sullen old nigger. She touched his arm, and spoke to him as if he were a child, without kindness.

"Don't you think you'd better have hot milk, instead of that coffee, Julie?"

He really looked at her then for the first time since he had come into the kitchen, suddenly annoyed with her because he felt he had failed with the old negress, and couldn't understand why.

"Look, Mary. Stop fussing," he told her. "You'd think I was on my last legs! It's coming down here, it never does you any good. You..."

"I've only got one grandmother." Mary Margaret found it as easy as breathing to slip into the natural blackmail of the remark, and was surprised at herself.

"Don't start that," Julik almost laughed at her; "I've never been through anything like that damned funeral. This place—geez—— Did you get a look at those aunts of yours, all like Hamlet's mother, assuming virtues...?" he leaned forward ready to dissect the experience with her, be objective, play at details, exorcise it with a good laugh.

But Mary Margaret said, "Shut up," so quietly that Julik wasn't sure he'd heard her until she apologised.

"Oh, Julie, I'm sorry." She reached across the table

and let her hand rest on his, both of them together, white hands without sex, telling secrets—hers flaked and dried with wringing-water and air, his tubercular fingers, still. "I'm not making sense. Don't pay any attention to me."

He didn't. "I'm sorry," she'd said, in her high, swinging voice, which sounded so sweet, though her mouth drooped down at the sides with sadness like a sorry clown. Julik sniffed, taking in more of the kitchen.

"Something smells funny."

"I expect it's the odor of bacon dripping. A'nt Elemere's always got beans on."

A'nt Elemere interrupted with great dignity, "Hog fat don't make no odor. Only people makes odors. This here's jest a plain smell of hog fat. Shame you don't like it."

Julik didn't like it. He finished his coffee with a gulp. "I'm going upstairs to lie down."

Mary Margaret got up to follow him. "I'll come with you."

"No, Mary, don't. I can wipe my own nose." He went out through the dining-room door, leaving her standing.

"What in the world you had to go and marry that unriz biscuit for I don't know. I jest don't know." A'nt Elemere launched into what she considered to be her rightful set of opinions, mostly because she'd half raised the girl. "Look at you! Twenty-seven years old. Pretty, jist wasting yourself. You ain't half the size you was when you went up there; little old skitty witch . . ."

Mary Margaret turned on her, angry, but she didn't raise her voice: "I never asked your opinion, A'nt Elemere."

A'nt Elemere paid just enough attention to her to mutter again, so she only half heard, "Comin' back down here with a lot of Yankee words and talkin' like an Irish woman. . . ."

The Kiss of Kin

"You never heard an Irish woman talk in your life. You're just repeating all the nasty things you've heard about me and Julie from the family. Julie's sick. I have a terrible time making him look after himself. You don't try to understand, any of you. . . ." There were tears coming into Mary Margaret's voice, but she tried to stop them, and so stopped speaking at all, and turned her back on A'nt Elemere.

A'nt Elemere's eyes found the ceiling. "For the love of the Lamb, look who's climbin' up on her high horse!"

There was only one cure for high horse. "Here, you sit back down and have some more coffee." She sat Mary Margaret down again, gently, and poured for her, but went on complaining because she hadn't had her whole say and no amount of tears was going to stop it.

"Odor! I been keepin' you from makin' a jackass out of yourself for twenty-five years and you don't expect me to quit jest because that there railroad takes you up north too easy. Odor! Who ever heard tell!"

But Mary Margaret was no longer even listening. She sat with her eyes unlit, not seeing the coffee. A'nt Elemere's pottering got slower and slower, until finally she leaned, elbows akimbo, watching the empty yard out of the window, her stomach flat against the low cabinet. The kitchen seemed to have run down into some kind of false peace.

Abraham, having got over the shock of watching the straggling little procession wind out through the back gate when he had expected a large funeral, sat and stared after it all the way up the branch road to the hill. He moved at last, slowly, when it was out of sight, and got out of the car. As he walked round it to cross the creek, he saw the little boy fall flat, and stopped again.

Mary Margaret broke the silence in the kitchen.

"There's only one day like this in the whole of our lives."

A'nt Elemere went on watching out the window, wondering who the tall man was, leaning on his car across the creek, who obviously couldn't make up his mind whether to come in or not. She saw John Junior fall for the tenth time that day, and paid no attention, but answered Mary Margaret.

"Ours, honey, not nobody else's. They don't even know what's happened yet. Neb mind."

She blew out a great whistling breath and picked herself up to meet John Junior, who was screaming his way up to the side-porch.

"I hurt myself," he wailed; his face was streaked with dust and tears, and his mouth was wet and pink and stretched with fear. A'nt Elemere stooped, caught him, examined him, and began to fuss all in one continuous habitual gesture.

"When are you gonna outgrow makin' all that noise ever' time you graze yourself? Here, let me see! It ain't nothin'. Git on out of here." She pushed him back out of the screen-door, and he stood outside it, his hurt forgotten, gaping in.

It came suddenly to Mary Margaret, like a revelation!

"He ought to have had hot milk."

She jumped up from the table.

A'nt Elemere was disgusted. "You jest spoil that man rotten, Mary Margaret, I ain't never seen the like of it. It ain't good for men to be fetched and carried for like you do him."

Mary Margaret was already putting milk on to heat. She knew it was no good being as furious as she felt with A'nt Elemere, with all of them for that matter, so she was deadly patient.

"A'nt Elemere, you just can't ever understand a man like Julie. None of you people down here could ever understand him. A'nt Elemere, he's a genius! They aren't like other people. They're something to be cared for. Rare things."

She stooped, looking for a cup in the low cabinet. A'nt Elemere wasn't paying much attention to what the girl was saying. She took it for what it sounded like, an apology for heating milk for a grown man in the afternoon.

"How could any of you understand?" Mary Margaret went on, explaining defensively. "I'll bet you've never heard anybody play the violin at all, much less lose himself in Brahms the way Julie can. Why he's . . ."

A'nt Elemere had had enough. "Your milk's boilin'," she said ungraciously, not bothering to take it off for Mary Margaret.

Mary Margaret rushed to grab it where it spread over the gas flame, and pour what was left in the cup she'd found, moaning a little.

"Oh, what a shame! Julie hates it with scum on it." She went out, still fussing a little in her soft way, through the empty house.

"Git away from that door. Quit that hangin' around my skirts. Go on." A'nt Elemere got rid of John Junior, who scuttled off down the path, almost knocking into a strange man. He turned then to stare, offering no information. Behind him in the kitchen, A'nt Elemere began to talk, strictly to herself.

"Well, ain't that jest too bad?" she started, banging Mary Margaret's cup and saucer down into the sink. "For the love of the Lamb, maybe I never did hear nobody play the fiddle like what he can, but by golly I know a nocount when I see one. Lord's love, I done seen enough of 'em around here in my time, so's I got some experience of 'em."

CHAPTER III

SO, as he'd always been told he would, Abraham Passmore, having stepped aside to avoid John Junior, heard A'nt Elemere's voice laying down the law in the kitchen as soon as he set foot on the back porch. At first he hesitated, then when he saw through the screen-door that she was alone, he let her rave, enjoying it, leaning at last up against the door-jamb, waiting for her to discover him.

"We done raised more pure-bred nocounts up this here creek than you could shake a stick at. He don't like scum! Hunh! Poor white trash! He oughta know about scum. It jest beats me the way my Mary Margaret done turn herself into some kind of nurse for that nocount!"

Then she saw the stranger, standing in the shadow side of the back door.

"How long you been standin' there?" She jerked open the screen-door to peer at him, slowly registering his height, the Passmore slant set of his eyes, the wide Passmore cheek-bones, the big mouth, the curiously feminine tilted chin. "Lord God Holy Jesus! Come in here! I know you!" Her voice was already filling with surprised tears; she pulled him into the sun.

"But I don't know you." She felt a sudden sick twinge of disappointment at the mistake she'd made; then she understood and brightened up again. "Oh Lord! If it ain't a miracle happened too late! Ain't you little Abraham?"

"Yes. Abraham's son."

A'nt Elemere was beside herself with joy.

"Well, I'll declare, you're the spittin' image. The spit of your paw. Sit down and have some coffee."

She sat him down carefully at the kitchen table, as if she were afraid he would disappear into the shadows again, and went on to tell him:

"You wouldn't remember your grandmaw, honey, but she passed over, Glory Jesus, two days ago. Here's some cream. She'd of jest given anything to see you walk in that door."

She stood watching him. "Young Abraham! Well, I'll declare! Same big bones. Same hair. Well, I'll declare!"

Abraham interrupted to answer the news about Miss Anna Mary, "I know about my grandmother. That's why I came."

"You're jest too late, unless you want to go on up to the grave-yard. They've opened the vault up there and they're layin' her in beside your grandpaw. Now you wouldn't of ever seen him. He died before you was born. He was a fair-size man, too," she added, taking in the breadth of Abraham's shoulders approvingly. Then she asked sadly, "Whyn't your daddy come, honey?"

"I'm standing for my part of the family," Abraham told her; then realising that he sounded already like a lawyer-called meeting, he changed the subject, grinning. "No. I don't think I'll go up to the grave-yard. I watched them all on the way in."

A'nt Elemere was curious, curious and worried. "Did any of 'em see you?"

"No," he caught the worry and reassured her. "They were being so sanctimonious they missed me." He was bitter. "I picked out every one of them from the stories I'd heard."

She chose not to see the bitterness, not yet. She was too pleased to see him. She almost crooned. "Well, what do you know? You was took away from here when you was knee-high."

"It was all hearsay. I don't claim to remember much."

Mary Margaret swept open the dining-room door and she stooped down to search in the cabinet under the sink without having seen Abraham, scrabbling through it with both hands, setting bandage, Flit, a can of Three-in-One oil out on to the floor.

"Is there any poultice in here?"

A'nt Elemere watched her, wondering at her panic. "I don't know, honey; what do you want it for?" Then, anxiously, "You ain't hurt yourself?"

"No. We've had an accident, though. Julie threw his hand back when he lay down on the bed, and hit the knob of that old brass bedstead. I would have thought they'd have gotten rid of it long ago. It's going to swell if we don't poultice it, and Julie's got an audition next week. It just can't swell! A'nt Elemere, please help me find some poultice."

A'nt Elemere didn't move. "You try some horse-linament," she advised.

"A'nt Elemere, this isn't just a hand. It's one of the tools of Julie's trade."

Abraham had got over his surprise at being interrupted by a neat little city girl as out of place there as a pug-dog. He smiled at the self-conscious excuse for art that went with the home-made, brave little dirndle. He'd heard it so often, so many places, but never before trotted out to apologise to somebody's cook in a way-to-hell-and-gone kitchen next to nowhere.

"Oh, I can't find a thing in here. Why can't you be some use?" She straightened up, and saw Abraham.

"Who are you?" She was rude with embarrassment, and couldn't stop staring at him. At first glance she took him for a man in an advertising company, because he seemed so young to be wearing such a well-cut suit. Then she remembered where she was, and was conscious of being out of context somehow—confused. All the time A'nt Elemere was explaining in her own terms, which she did with gusto.

"This here's your, now lemme see, your second cousin, once remove, same kin as Mary Armstrong and John Junior to you. This here's Abraham!"

"Abraham?" Mary Margaret was too startled to keep the words from slipping out. "Why, I never thought you'd . . ."

"You never thought you'd see one of my lot here again. Is that it? Seems you were wrong." He grinned at her, a lazy, 'squatter's rights' grin.

She found his studied insolence so childish and out of place with the rest of his bearing that she saw him for a second as a double image, a brat in advertising man's clothing. It was not hard for her to see which kept control most of the time, for his fine clothes were still uncreased after what must have been a long, hot drive and his general air of almost ruthless self-assurance and poise seemed to bring him into focus and tell her who was boss, even as she watched him. But even so, there was his brave little-boy mouth, a stern slit, as if he'd fixed it that way once to keep himself from trembling like a sissy, and then had let it become a habit. Mary Margaret felt a twinge of disgusted awareness of that mouth.

But all she could muster to say to him was:

"I think you're . . ." What she really thought he was she never said, because A'nt Elemere interrupted, as proud as an old hen.

Mary Margaret forgot to go on looking for the poultice. She just stood there while A'nt Elemere remembered her whole history.

"This here's Mary Margaret. Her maw, the one you'd

call A'nt Mary Lee, is daughter to Miss Anna Mary's half-sister by some man name of Elecky." She obviously disapproved of this union, made sixty years before. "She ain't really your a'nt. He come from up some creek. Miss Mary Lee married a Longridge." But she did not disapprove of this one. *A Longridge*, she'd called him, not *one of them*, or worse, *some*. "That's Mary Margaret's paw. He ain't dead yet, but he's pore. Been that way for years. Had something like fifteen stomach operations. Mary Margaret lived here when she was a youngin. Miss Anna Mary that she calls her granmaw ain't her grandmaw atall, but her great a'nt." Now the history ended with deep disgust. "After Mary Margaret growed up, she went up north and married some man."

Abraham, wanting to upset this silly girl who stood as balanced as a plate on the edge of a table, asked, to stop her gawping at him, "Is that your kid who's hurt his hand?"

"No, my husband. It's my husband." She found herself explaining, not wanting to, but doing it anyway. "It's my husband. He's a violinist, so, you see, he must be terribly careful of his hands."

But Julik flung the dining-room door against the wall with his shoulder, and now he came in, holding the hurt hand in the other like an egg. He saw that Mary Margaret was doing nothing, just standing in the shadow, staring at a stranger.

"Mary!"

"I've got to go now," she apologised to the man, hardly hearing him call.

"Oh, Mary, haven't you fixed anything yet? Please, you know how important it is."

Abraham walked between them, taking the hand in his own, looking it over. "Let me see."

"Be careful. Don't touch the swelling. Are you another member of the family? My name's Rosen."

Abraham looked up. "I don't see any swelling. Yes, I'm a member."

Julik was disappointed. "I guess you think I'm making too much of it." He tried to grin apologetically through his worry. "Did Mary tell you I'm a violinist?" He kneaded his hand and winced. "It hurts like hell."

It was impossible for Mary Margaret not to compare them, standing together, both looking at Julik's hand. Julik's more intense face, with its long thin jaw, and the high backward sweep of his hair, gave him a softer, gentler look compared to the squarer, browner face so close to him, a face more cruel, and more naïve, than his had ever been. A'nt Elemere, on the other hand, compared them without any qualms. To her, as she beamed at Abraham and then wiped her face quite blank to look at Julik, Julik was nothing but a long, pale drink of water, and Abraham Passmore was simply the way a man of the family ought to be.

Abraham, sensing the scrutiny of the women, did what he thought they expected of him. He took over, began to give orders.

"Well, the best thing you can do is to soak it in salt water for a while. Here," Abraham went to the sink, moving as easily in the room as if he'd always known it, and poured out a dish-pan of hot water. "Where's some salt?"

A'nt Elemere handed it to him, because he was Abraham, not because she approved.

"That'll keep the swelling from coming at all. Sit down here."

Julik obeyed, and Abraham took his hand gently and put it in the water. "Now don't move it out until I tell you to."

Julik watching his hand settle, remembered to look up and smile his thanks. Sitting undulating his hand through the water, he was comforted, and bursting with talk. "There's something absolutely nerve-racking about this house." He looked up at Abraham. "Have you noticed it yet? It fascinates me, but I can't stand it. Mary, could we possibly leave by the five o'clock train?"

"Julie, you know we can't." Her voice, despite herself, took on a slight note of secrecy. "We've got to stay this evening," Mary Margaret went on, tired of telling him, tired of the whole damn thing.

Julik ignored her warning. "Have I soaked it long enough yet?" he asked Abraham.

"No."

He went on, waving his hand through the water, watching it, thinking aloud. "Why can't you have a talk with the lawyer when they come back and tell him I've got to get away?"

Mary Margaret turned her back, hoping to stop him. "I don't think that would make much difference. Cousin Cad thought too much of grandmaw. I think he's awfully upset at having to read her will on the day she's buried anyway." Then she found herself explaining to Abraham. "But everybody thought it best . . ."

Abraham, realising what the fuss was about, said to A'nt Elemere, "Well, look at the little kittens in for their share of meat," and laughed at his joke, not caring that A'nt Elemere didn't laugh with him.

Mary Margaret knew more about him then. "You've just come down here to make trouble, haven't you?" she said. Suddenly she was annoyed, because he was there at all and because she had hoped to go through this day carried by the strangeness of formal events and reactions in a place she knew so well; carried through it like dead

Miss Anna Mary under her trembling pall of rosebuds. She had hoped to end up on the train to New York, shuttling through the dark, and then wake up, far away enough by then to be safe. But here this man had come, who she knew wasn't the kind who'd let sleeping dogs lie.

"I think the best you could do, Abraham, when we're all so upset, is to come with the right attitude to our feelings." In her anger she sounded so like her mother instead of her gentle self that A'nt Elemere started up, surprised.

But it was Abraham who interrupted—"Oh, I have, kid. I'm a real funeral pie—" and ruined her moment of righteous anger by suddenly laughing out loud again.

The noise of it aroused Julik from weaving the water around the bowl. He thought from the laughter that Abraham was taking it all as lightly as he did, and went on to explain to him, "Maybe it's because I can't wait any longer that I'm so on edge today. If you could only realise all the time we've been hanging around . . ."

Mary Margaret heard him, and her anger vanished. She felt a wave of happiness, like a sudden temperature. "Never mind, Julie," she told him, as tenderly as if they'd been alone. "It won't be long now."

He paid no attention, but went on dreaming and weaving the water. Something in his own mind, or in Mary Margaret's words, had touched off a wave of bitterness he made no attempt to stop.

"If you had any idea what it's like. People of no talent went past me. All the goddamned snobs ignored me. Not that they matter, but you know . . . The number of times I stood around and watched a lot of fools . . ." He was still for a minute, aware that he himself was being watched too closely at the moment. So he tried to make a joke of it. "Who said money doesn't talk? I ought to know."

Mary Margaret interrupted, "Julik, why don't you . . . just shut up?"

Abraham and A'nt Elemere were too embarrassed to say a word.

Without looking up at her, just hearing Mary Margaret's voice, Julik knew he had made a terrible error.

"Do you have to talk to me like that in front of other people, Mary?" he said, mild with patience.

A'nt Elemere threw in her two-cents' worth: "Seems to me you're talkin' pretty free yourself," she snarled.

Julik was angry, mostly because he was a little shamed and frightened at being in the centre of a lack of ease where no one was daring to look at anyone else. "Oh, I suppose it embarrasses you because I talk about the things that matter to me! I suppose you think a man's dreams are embarrassing in a bourgeois society like this. All you goddamn people with your goddamn polite breeding. Why does everything always turn shameful to people like you?" He was suddenly furious. "I was raised in a slum. Do you have an idea what that means? Do you know? It means ambition, the kind you people don't know about —when you're raised on nothing, in a slum." He had taken his hand out of the water, but now he put it back and sat silent.

A'nt Elemere crowed, seeing it all, "Wait till you hear these here people git to tearin' at each other over that there will with their maw not cold in her grave, and you'll git a bellyful of polite breedin' to remember 'em by!"

Julik's voice went low in a solemn litany. "We never had quite enough to eat."

Abraham interrupted quietly, to shut him up, "Lots of people haven't. I didn't."

A'nt Elemere was horrified. "Abraham, honey, what are you sayin'? Lemme make you a samich!"

Abraham grinned at her, "Never mind, A'nt Elemere."

"You eben knowed my name!"

"From Mary Margaret. But I was told all about you." He talked fast to cover for the humiliated man sitting at the table. "I was told I'd walk up to that door and that I'd hear you laying down the law inside; it wouldn't make any difference whether there was anybody else in the kitchen or not. I was told you'd be laying it down anyway. You were. I won't say what about." Then he forgot why he had begun to talk, and slipped over into being hang-dog and boyish. "I was told you were the only decent person in this house."

A'nt Elemere knew ahead there would be trouble. "Well, son, you wasn't told quite right there. Not quite right," was all she said.

"I'll decide about that." He turned to the screen-door and looked out into the side-yard.

"Haven't I had it in long enough now?" Julik called Abraham back into the room, grateful to him and afraid of losing him for an ally.

"What? Yes, long enough." Julik couldn't tell by that whether Abraham was still sympathetic or not. It made him awkward, made him slow down a little. He prodded his dripping hand, kneaded it, excited. "It's gone! The pain's disappeared. Hand me a towel, Mary."

She had already found one, and held it ready for him.

"Oh, how can I thank you enough? It was very nice of you to take so much trouble with me. Wasn't it thoughtful of him, Mary?"

She only heard her name. "What?"

Julik had hoped she'd forgotten. But when she spoke he realised he'd still have to deal with her, caught on a point and needing dislodging.

"Mary, for God's sake, can't you get your mind off that

point? When I'm successful, all that will work of its own accord. . . ." He forgot there was anyone else in the room, and begged her to see. "Can't you see I'm right, Mary? You're just a woman; you can't imagine what this all means to me. Try not to be so selfish!"

Mary Margaret was lodged, stubborn, hurt.

"You don't know what the other means to me."

Abraham there, sizing him up with every word, A'nt Elemere, watching him flat-eyed with dislike, were not enough to stop Julik. Too much was at stake. "Look at it this way, Mary. Here's the tag-end of a family, about to fall apart anyway. Here they have a chance to help somebody who's really worth it. Jesus, what have they ever done before? Look at it that way, please, Mary. God knows after all my effort I deserve it." He so believed it that for a second Mary Margaret saw beyond her own hurt and was almost persuaded.

"I see . . ." she began.

A'nt Elemere exploded. "Well, I doesn't! I disremember when I ever heard such . . ."

"Stop it! Stop it!" Mary Margaret was so near to tears that her voice made the other two begin to move towards the door, even before she ordered. "Stay out of this for once. Abraham, A'nt Elemere, please go on out, both of you. Please!"

Abraham took A'nt Elemere's arm and piloted her unwilling bulk out of the screen-door to the edge of the porch. "Come on, A'nt Elemere, let them alone."

The door slammed behind them, and they stood teetering on the porch edge, squinting into the sun.

"Why the Lord everybody has to use my kitchen to do their fussin' in—always did do it—lettin' the beans burn . . ." A'nt Elemere mumbled and ended with a grunt, too disgusted to be bothered with any more words.

The Kiss of Kin

"We better stay out on the porch, anyway." Abraham still kept tight hold of her arm.

"We kin hear jest as good out here."

But Mary Margaret's voice was so quiet with a new surge of fury when she took in the full insult of Julik's argument that they could hear only a murmur, and the rhythm of her talking. Then her voice rose until the words could be made out: "Don't you ever let me hear that kind of talk about my people again." Her voice subsided and went on murmuring. Julik had not said a word.

A'nt Elemere darted down the side-yard when she saw what John Junior was up to.

"John Junior, you let that dog alone!"

She caught him in front of the smoke-house.

"I didn't do nothin'!" he yelled. A'nt Elemere slapped him hard.

In the kitchen Julik had managed to interrupt at last, and had pulled Mary Margaret down into a chair, putting his arm round her, leaning over her.

"Now listen to me, darling. Listen. Are you listening to me?" He waited judiciously until he had caught her curiosity and made her nod. Then he spoke carefully as a mother or a doctor. "You know it's bad for you to come down here, don't you? You shed all this stifling family thinking until you come back. Then the phrases creep in, and you can't see straight or think straight. You know I'm right, don't you?"

It hadn't had quite the right effect. She started to wave her hands in the air, explaining, trying to make him see. "I know you're right, but you're not right for the right reasons, Julik. Don't you see that? You don't try to understand these people at all." She ended in a wail, and the last 'all' was nearly sung.

But she had only turned Julik back to the isolation of

his own perpetual anger. "When did they start trying to understand me?" Anger enough to take the lid off the argument and come to the point at last. "But skip that. Let's get to the point. Nobody's mentioned Ethel yet. You know you only want to spend a lot of money on a divorce that's six years overdue because of some kind of phoney sensibility you pick up when you come back down here. I wish to God you'd listen to me and stay away. It's poison for you."

Julik had begun, long before he finished with the truth of the matter, to pace up and down the room, gesticulating, being logical, making points with his hands flat and sensible against the hot air of the kitchen. Any place else it would have worked: in the kitchen of their apartment on West 83rd Street with yesterday's *Herald Tribune* always on the floor for the dog, in the only really good Italian restaurant they'd found and been loyal to in New York, at Bill's place down-town, or Bertie's up-town, everybody would have joined in and had an interesting discussion. But here, Jesus, the girl was a stranger, his own docile Mary Margaret; here in a hot and unimportant kitchen with the past spun round her like a thickening chrysalis of old attitudes, old fears he couldn't understand.

Mary Margaret was hardly even listening to him. She sat, rocking slightly, her thin arms crossed in her lap, her fingers weaving without her being aware of any movements. "We hadn't decided. We hadn't decided," she kept repeating, like a little girl, cheated.

"Don't go stubborn on me, Mary. Jesus, you're not a baby any more!"

"The concert or a divorce from Ethel," she said flatly, looking at him at last. "How many times we've talked it over, planned first one and then the other like some couples plan a house or a family. You were only fooling me, all the time. You'd already made up your mind. Julie, you ought to be ashamed of yourself. I wouldn't have lived with you without marrying you unless I'd thought you would do something about it as soon as you could."

She looked so like a quietly scolding little teacher that Julik capitulated and made an excuse to fit her mood. "We're married in the sight of God, honey."

Mary Margaret had a sudden desire to grin, like a spasm of her mouth. "I want to be married to you in the sight of man, Julie. I always have." She threw off her tired primness in a panic. "It even makes me sick at my stomach. You know it makes me sick at my stomach," she accused.

"Look, Mary." Julik had had enough. "Aren't you being a little babyish? Did I ever say I wouldn't do something as soon as I could?"

Mary Margaret had veered away already. He couldn't catch up with her. She begged, as if that was what they'd been talking about: "Julik, please, please, help me!"

Julik couldn't help then but be very tender with her. She was obviously too upset to make sense. This time she felt his arm across her shoulders.

"Who's upset my girl this much? There's something else, isn't there, honey?"

He lulled her into admitting what it really was. "It's Mama. She knows, and she's just been watching me like a cold fish ever since we got here."

Julik patted her. "You're probably imagining it, darling. Don't think I don't sympathise. I'm scared of her too." He laughed a little.

"It's painful." Mary Margaret sighed, her head against his shoulder. But the position was giving him a crick in his back, so he stood upright and let her go.

"Well, you try to forget it. Don't make things up. Christ, you're a big girl now. What could she do to you?"

He thought, when she didn't answer, couldn't put fear into words, that it was all over and made right. "Now everything's O.K., isn't it?" He started out of the room to have his rest at last. "I'm going to lie down." A new thought made him turn, worried. "Do you think they all noticed when I didn't go to the grave-yard?"

He had withdrawn his sympathy too soon and he left her stranded, panicked, as if he had closed a door and shut out the light. She could only be as waspish as she knew how.

"I'm sure they didn't notice, Julik. We've had a death in the family. We don't notice much right now." Her mood had already switched again. "Now that man's turned up. I don't know . . ."

"I'm going upstairs until you're in a saner mood. I'm fed up." He went out, slamming the door.

CHAPTER IV

MARY MARGARET put her head down on the table and began to cry, letting the tears fall, with her head almost in them, not because of an old problem, a decision, a quarrel, or even a death of someone she loved, but just because of being caught and made to wake up in the middle of a hot afternoon. But too much trouble had made her dull with sleepiness. When she heard the screen-door open behind her, she thought it was A'nt Elemere.

"A'nt Elemere, gimme a cup of coffee...." She rolled her head back and forth between her arms to cool her face.

Abraham answered her, hardly hearing her muffled voice, walking up close behind her. "She's down with a stick after the boy. Just to make herself feel better, she said."

She forgot that she'd been crying in her surprise at being caught by Abraham, and looked up at him, curious, ready to yawn.

"What did you come here for?"

"Oh, I don't know. I guess I thought I'd find out a few things...."

"Why you weren't mentioned? Why you never came here before?"

"Maybe. Do you know anything about it?"

She decided he was being sly, and answered him as formally as she could. "No. I only know your father was a relative I never saw. No mention of anything."

"And about her?" He wasn't looking at her.

"Who?"

"My mother." Then he was, and she found she couldn't protect herself by being dignified.

"Nothing about her. Never." She was so near him that they found themselves almost whispering to each other. He walked away from her, not liking the intimacy, and raised his voice. "A'nt Elemere will know. That black witch will know. I'll get her alone. Some way I thought you'd tell me."

"You think I know."

Abraham was not whispering any longer. "I know damn well you do. When something happens in a house like this, everybody knows. It seeps out from behind closed doors. The children take trouble into their skin. There was some kind of trouble. O.K. So you won't tell me."

"I don't know. Maybe I wasn't here yet. It must have been a long time ago, whatever it was."

"Over twenty-five years ago."

"I wasn't here yet. That long ago? How in the world could it still matter to you?"

He defended himself with more violence than her question needed, because he wasn't quite sure himself why. "It matters to me. Leave it at that, will you? You'd have told me if you'd known, wouldn't you?" He was still suspicious of her.

"Of course I'd have told you. What do you think?"

He went close to her again. "I think this house is woman crazy. If I hadn't seen them all ploughing up the holy path, I'd swear one of them was listening behind every door!"

"It's only the buzz of the flies you hear. They drive you wild if you stop to listen."

"They will all gather this evening to discuss property. I can't wait." He smiled to himself, thinking of the women.

"So that's why you've come?"

He smoothed the oil-cloth of the table with his flat hand, leaning down to her. "I was sent for." Satisfied at her surprise, he stood up again.

"Why didn't your father come?"

"It was me they sent for." He seemed to be listening, but not to her. "When I was a kid I used to dream that a big house like this was on fire. I used to hide so nobody would find out it was me who burned it."

He wandered round the room, touching the furniture, the coal-range by the dining-room door, past the door itself. He opened it a fraction, and, seeing and smelling the high-banked flowers in the oven-hot dining-room, closed it again. He passed the sink with its damp drain-board under the sunny window, paused to drum his fingers over the dirty screen of the door to the side-yard, where beyond the big pine tree the smoke-house, the milk-house, the corn-bin and the chicken-run that he'd seen leaning towards the creek looked now like a toy street, and were casting long shadows across the yard to the kitchen porch. He even looked idly inside the low cabinet under the second big window which matched the sink window and made the side of the kitchen like a huge cage.

"I can't remember as much as I thought I could, now that I see it." He stopped in front of the second screen-door to the back gate where he'd come in first, and leaned beside it, watching nothing, remembering. "The flutter of white dresses is something I'll never forget. Oh, and the sound of women's voices going higher and higher sounding like a lot of squabbling chickens. I left here in my pyjamas, all wrapped up in a blanket. I remember because I was scared someone would see me going on the train like that...."

He turned to inspect the kitchen cabinet, touching along

the enamelled tin surface as if he were trying to charm some memory out of it.

"It all looks so damned different, though."

"Didn't your parents tell you anything?"

"Nothing much. I picked up remarks, naturally. But not enough. Never enough to show me what really happened here. Whatever it was, I hated it. I used to come in the house from school and realise the minute I hit the door when they'd been talking about it, turning it over, both of them edgy." He was still for so long she thought he'd finished. Then he added, "I still hate it, whatever it is."

He turned finally, coming back into the room to where she sat. "I came to find out about it, if you want to know the truth."

She wanted to giggle at him because he was so naïve, and he talked too much, and he was being drawn in, just like some damn man, more than he had any idea of. All the big talk. She couldn't stop herself, realised how numb she felt in the middle of the slight giggle which had slipped out and turned it into a yawn.

"Oh, excuse me. It's the day." She tried to apologise, and yawned again.

"What were you laughing at? Haven't I got a right..."

"Sure. Sure, you've got a right, Abraham. It's just happening again, that's all."

"What?"

"The house. It's got you, too, but you've not even been here since you were two or three years old."

He saw the yawn begin again, the girl helpless, involved in numb, hot desire for sleep, and did the first thing he knew to wake her up. He picked her up from her chair, kissed the funny mouth which made her look so childish, and then held her head, tight, in his hands, while she stared. Then he said the other thing that had been on his mind.

"Why, you're not in love with that man!"

"You stop. Stop that!" She tried to turn her head away, but he held her.

"You told me so." Abraham was triumphant. She didn't try to move away from him then, only stood there, studying his face.

"You are down here to destroy this house," she decided and told him solemnly.

"I will destroy this house." It was his turn to laugh at her, mimicking her. "Cousin Mary Margaret, you're too little to act so damned solemn." This time he held her close, talking into her hair. "Let's you and me stick together. We'll open the cupboards and take down the books, clean out the smoke-house, rattle the bones . . ."

Mary Margaret giggled, this time sharing the joke, cosy against his chest.

Over her shoulder, he looked out of the screen-door to the back gate. A little huddle of people had gathered there, saying good-bye. Two figures in black turned towards the house, head down. He could just hear one of them say, as she turned, "No. There's nothing you can do. It's all done."

"Here come the big cats," Abraham whispered, then, with a quick compassion at the tiredness and lifelessness of the two women coming up the path, he added, "They'd better know I'm here before they see me," and disappeared through the dining-room door towards the front of the house.

CHAPTER V

MARY LEE and Amelia filed past Mary Margaret without speaking, as she ran to hold the door open for them, wiping her mouth. Some of the dignity of the funeral hung about them as they drooped; that, and exhaustion from standing in black clothes too long in the sun.

Amelia collapsed into a chair and took her hat off to fan herself with it. Mary Lee stopped, rigid, in the middle of the room, intent, as if she were trying to remember why she came into the kitchen at all.

Mary Margaret walked back to her, letting the door swing behind her. She knew from the stance, from the greyness of her mother's face, from the way she had seen her sweep her hand across her eyes, that by midnight Mary Lee would be pacing the cool attic with the migraine tightening around her head. She knew too that by morning the thin sick wreck of her would be over it, in what was for her the rare state of being weak and vulnerable, moving carefully about like a woman who has been blind drunk.

"Mother," she tried to sympathise, to jar her from her frozen position in the middle of the kitchen. But she had gone too close without warning. Mary Lee turned, savagely, using the voice and the slam of the screen-door to release her sorrow, which had by now turned to anger. "Why weren't you at the grave? Why didn't you come on after me?"

"I couldn't, Mother. I just couldn't."

"What do you mean by flaunting yourself the way you're doing?" Mary Lee's attack veered to what was really on her mind.

44

The Kiss of Kin

"I don't know what you mean," Mary Margaret defended herself, feeling hot with fear like a caught little girl because she'd been kissed by Abraham and her mother might have seen it.

"What I may and may not mean has nothing to do with it!" Mary Lee's shrill voice was as much to the point as her words irrelevant; she accused Mary Margaret in little gasps, fighting for air in her stiff corset of a chest. "I don't know how much you're trying to hide from me, but let me tell you, if you bring that man you're living with in fornication down here any more, there'll be a different kind of welcome. We're decent people."

"Oh, Mother, is that what you're talking about? Julik?"

"I can't pronounce his name. What are these people to think?"

"Oh, Mother, why can't you believe anything I say? You ought to try and understand. Julik and I are married!"

"In the sight of God, I suppose! You always were exactly right, Mary Margaret; always had a fine excuse for yourself."

"Mother, please don't . . ." Mary Margaret would have said one of the sympathetic phrases she knew would help to stop the tirade '. . . upset yourself any more . . . worry yourself with all you've got to do . . .' but Mary Lee cut her off, her voice edged and shrill.

"Don't talk to me any more. You upset me so much I can't stand it." She rushed by her out of the room.

Mary Margaret forgot her as soon as she had gone. The repetition had become long since a kind of dope, where she could close her mind at the sound of her mother's voice. Now she stepped in the same place her mother had stood, wondering where she wanted to go to rest, and found herself yawning again.

The Kiss of Kin

When Amelia had relieved herself by pulling her corset out from her flabby thighs and releasing a puff of air, she went to the kitchen cabinet. "Where's some soda? I need some soda," she talked to herself, rummaging through the cabinet, expecting Mary Margaret to overhear her excuse. But Mary Margaret only asked, "Where's A'nt Cinnybug?"

"She's out there in the back-yard talking to your Uncle Jelly. Lord knows what they've got to talk about after twenty-five years. I reckon Cinny just wears everybody else out, talking so much as she has, to finish up with Jelly."

She found what she wanted, turned the bottle up behind the door of the kitchen cabinet, and drank. With a heaving sigh she sat down again, dusting and blowing the flour from her black sleeve. She flopped back and let herself be sad again.

"You'll get used to it, days like this, Mary Margaret," she began to reminisce softly, feeling a cosier sadness as the drink blossomed inside her. "I remember when your Uncle Charles was taken. It was a day just like this. A hot day, with this kind of sleepy afternoon, the day of the funeral. Do you remember Uncle Charles?"

The memory of Charles Truxton Edwards had been more present in the house than ever Charles himself had; Mary Margaret could not remember a time when any happening had not been seen for Amelia as only a stick to stir up memories of the past she half lived in.

"No, ma'am, I don't think so," Mary Margaret answered, hoping, just today, to stop her.

But Amelia was launched into her story. "Well, there, you never would have seen him more than two or three times. It's too bad. Charles Truxton Edwards was a very fine man. A very fine man."

Mary Margaret softened toward her plump, sad cousin. The day and the hopeful dread of the coming evening had not isolated her, as it had most of the others, stranded in their own desires, waiting. Instead her senses seemed to yearn for contact, and she found herself wanting to listen to Amelia. "Were you so happy with him?" she asked the old lone bore.

"Happy, honey?" Amelia interrupted her, wondering. "Of course I was happy. You're happy when you're married, aren't you?" She began to dream again. "We had a little house with a front- and back-yard. It was the cutest little old thing you ever saw. We lived in Tennessee, just over the North Carolina border. Charles Truxton's work took him there. He was in tobacco. Happy! I should say I was!"

"A'nt Amelia, tell me something. Sometimes . . . did you forget you were in love with Uncle Charles?" She leaned hopefully on her arms, watching, asking for more of the theme song, hoping for guidance as women rustle until they find the Sunday horoscope in the newspaper, clutching anywhere for certainty.

"Never for a minute of the day or night, honey. It's my happy memory. It's what I live on now."

Amelia belched carefully, and hoisted herself in her chair. "Excuse me," she murmured, then brightened. "Let me tell you about our house . . ."

But Mary Margaret had had her answer, and she was in danger of crying again because of it, so she pushed open the screen-door and called over her shoulder, "Some other time, A'nt Amelia, I'd like to hear all about it . . ." and ran off down the side-yard away from the women's voices.

Mary Lee kicked open the dining-room door and elbowed herself through it, grasping in both hands a bowl of tight, waxy, long-stemmed roses, wired so tightly they stuck up like long quills. She set them in the sink, and twisted the cold water tap until the water splashed hard over them.

"Who was that went out?" she called over the noise of the water.

Amelia didn't bother to bend round to look at her, but she knew better than not to answer, "Mary Margaret," already weary and bored again.

Mary Lee craned her neck to take in as much of the side-yard as she could from the window. "Humph! Running off towards the creek. I reckon she's going to enjoy a good cry. She always did when she went down to the creek. That girl sure is one to hug her own miseries." She slapped at the screen. "This place is just alive with flies! Where's the Flit?"

She bent down to the cabinet under the sink, taking out the Flit gun. It was then that Amelia saw the flowers. "What are those things doing in here?" She could hardly find her voice to ask. She sat, frozen, as if she were in a nightmare and couldn't wake up to scream. So what she said was whispered, but Mary Lee heard enough to turn and look, and then ignore the silly woman.

She started to 'Flit' the room furiously instead, as if there were virtue in it. "Well, somebody had to look after them." She offered the information while she sprayed the air. "It might as well be me. It always is in the long run. There wasn't room for them on the coffin and there's no use to waste them."

Amelia watched them, as if she expected them to come alive, coil, and strike at her. She managed to whisper again, "Mary Lee, please get them out of here."

Mary Lee stopped attacking the flies and stood in front of her, watching. "What are you going on for?"

"They make me feel sick," Amelia whispered, and begged, "Please, Mary Lee, take them out again!"

The Kiss of Kin

"Well, I never saw such goings-on over a little vase of flowers."

Mary Lee swept over to the sink, shut off the water, and wrenched the dripping vase up into her hands. "You're just nothing but a damn fool, Amelia."

She carried the flowers over and set them down in the middle of the kitchen table.

"There!" wiping her hands on her skirt, "I'm putting them right there and don't you act like such a fool. There's not any use to waste them and they'll just die out in the dining-room with nobody to see them."

At first Amelia was too frightened by the flowers, set almost under her nose, to move at all. Then she started up. "Take them away, Mary Lee, I warn you I can't stand it."

"I never saw such damn foolishness in all my born days. Just over a little bunch of flowers!"

Mary Lee grabbed Amelia's arm tightly as she finally struggled out of her chair and tried to pass.

"You're not going out because of them! You've been drinking licker all day, that's what's the matter with you, damn you, Amelia!"

"Let go of me!" Amelia pulled away from Mary Lee; still not looking at her, but only at the flowers, she staggered through the dining-room door.

Mary Lee, having said what was on her mind, moved busily and almost happily, getting the kitchen in order again. She took the few cups off the table, put them in the sink, marched to the stove to 'look at' the beans, jiggled the heavy iron pan belligerently. Then she swept it up and struggled with it to the sink.

A'nt Elemere saw her as she heaved up the back stairs to the screen-door. "What chew doin' with them greenbeans?"

Mary Lee told her, over her shoulder, "I'm just putting a little water on them." She lifted the pan and staggered back to the stove with it. "They were set to burn. If you'd look after your own cooking once in a while, A'nt Elemere, it'd be a little added strain off my shoulders. Heaven knows I've got enough to worry me without you letting things burn all over the place."

"Well, I like to know when it woulda been polite for me to come in and stir my green-beans, please, in the last twenty minutes, with all the goings-on!"

"A'nt Elemere, don't you talk back to me." Mary Lee didn't wait to hear A'nt Elemere's answer. She had already gone into the front of the house, jabbing the door with her skinny, bony arm. A'nt Elemere made herself clear to nothing but the creak of the door as it swung behind her.

"I don't see why I can't ask a simple question once in a while. I know why. There just ain't no plain, simple people around this place to answer 'em." Then she laid eyes on those flowers.

"I'd like to know who put them store-bought flowers on my clean table. Well, they can jest go right back where they come from, that's all." She picked them up. "Look at that there ring!"

She swished the water from the table with her apron. "I ain't havin' no funeral blooms in my kitchen and that's all there is to it."

So, just as Mary Lee had brought them in, A'nt Elemere took the roses back again, her elbows akimbo to catch the door, into the empty dining-room which seemed to buzz with silence and be forgotten, now that the intensity of death had passed beyond it to other rooms, spread out as separate burdens as the family had wandered all over the house.

The long mahogany table had been pushed back against

the wall, and assorted chairs from the living-room, the bedrooms, as far away as the attic, were still set in snaggled uneven rows where people had leaned forward to pray or look or ease themselves. In the ten-foot-square space where Miss Anna Mary Passmore had rested in the early afternoon on a bank of rings and roses and half-moons of tight, long-lasting store-bought flowers, her old shrivelled head powdered and marcelled like a doll, there were now only three naked quilting trestles in a line. Behind them against the summer-sealed fireplace, a criss-cross of flower-stands leaned together looking like a sold-out church bazaar. A'nt Elemere put the flowers down on the flat oak sideboard, forgot them at once, and set to work gathering up the quilting horses to take them back to the attic, trying to restore the familiarity of the room again before she succumbed to its dead silence.

CHAPTER VI

CINNYBUG LAMB prissed up the back path, her voice going on as steady as breathing, talking to Jellicoe over her shoulder. She carried in her fast, bouncing walk the memory of a body that had once been cute, little and slim with dimpled knees, a beauty which by now everyone had forgotten. Her voice was a nostalgic caricature. Where it had been breathless, now it was edgy; the trill of expectation of her youth had long been replaced by a shrill apprehension. She still wore her hair bobbed; cut by the same barber in Palmyra who had always done it, finishing with the clippers. All of this meant to most of the unnoticing people around her that Cinnybug had changed least of any of them.

On the other hand Jellicoe, lounging behind her, had just about run down. He had grown querulous, the old candy-ankle, sorrowfully lazy, apologetically weary. He spoke somehow like a plump, ageing woman.

As Cinnybug went on with her hands in the air in front of her, Jellicoe looked as if he had long since stopped listening, but was following her with his head down, so that if she happened to glance his way, which she seldom did, she would suppose he was deep in thought about what he would answer, if he ever got a chance.

"Jellicoe, what do you think, I just want to know what you think that's all; after all, you've got to live in it too. . . ."

They reached the screen-door and walked into the now empty kitchen.

"If I take most of the furniture out of the living-room I feel lonesome with you gone so much and if I put it all back I feel cluttered when there's two of us in the room."

Jellicoe collapsed at the kitchen table, wiping the sweat from around his eyes.

"I don't know, honey, you gwan do whatever you want to." He yawned until his jaw creaked faintly.

"Jellicoe, I wish you'd take a little bit of interest in the house. I'll declare with all my worry and fussing over it I don't think you really look at it from one year's end to the next."

"Oh, I like it, honey, you gwan do whatever you want to; I'll like it." He began to finger his chin, and then round his mouth, thinking.

"What's gotten into you today, Jellicoe?" Cinnybug finally looked at him. "You're hardly listening to a word I say."

Jellicoe looked worried. "Nothing, Cinny, nothing. It's just hot, and I don't know whether I ought to have took the day off or not. You know what Mr. Crasscopper's like most of the time."

Cinnybug turned and began to search through the kitchen cabinet, uncovering plates, scrambling through the back for hidden things to eat.

"Mr. Crasscopper!" There was a world of new contempt in Cinny's voice. "After tonight we can say boo-turkey to Mr. Crasscopper." She smelt something in a tin, but made a little face and put it back.

She had surprised Jellicoe enough for him to take notice of what she said for once. He was shocked. "Why, Cinnybug, I wouldn't talk like that if I was you. You know Mr. Crasscopper's my boss."

She found a plate of cookies and began to 'taste' them, nibbling at the edges, and crumbling them thoughtfully in her lips. "He's more'n your boss," she told Jellicoe,

The Kiss of Kin

blowing a little cookie dust before her. "He's practically owned us for the last twenty-five years. Meely musta made these cookies. They've got more sugar than Mary Lee puts in."

"Cinnybug, you know times were hard right after that. Things never did pan out. Mr. Crasscopper's been pretty nice about that loan all these years. You ought to see how he treats some people."

In his weary way, Jellicoe told about the loan, as he'd told about it almost every day for years, saying the same words. By repetition he hardly heard them any more himself; Cinnybug didn't hear them at all, only the name, the name like a red flag that tilted at her, starting her off for the thousandth time.

"Jelly, there's one thing I just never can understand about you. You're scared to death of Mr. Crasscopper, and yet every day you have to go collecting money yourself. I'd be a lot scareder of people that owed money." Her voice slid on the word: Cinny said 'money' like a whiney little girl calling her mommy. She settled back and examined Jelly all over, her mouth hidden behind a cookie. "I reckon you're just scareder of Mr. Crasscopper than you are of them. Here, have a cookie."

"Now you leave me alone, Cinny. I know what you think of me, you needn't try and hide it."

"Gwan and try one," she interrupted, not questioning what he said; after all, she'd never tried to hide it, so the whole accusation was false.

"No, I don't want a damn cookie," Jelly wailed, explaining, "Now you listen to me, Cinnybug: you know it wasn't my fault and you know I've worked as hard as I could for the last twenty-five years."

"Why, honey, what's got your goat?" she worried at him; then sternly, "Jellicoe, have your bowels moved today?"

"Oh, Cinny, there isn't anything the matter. Mr. Crasscopper's been at me lately, and you know how it gets my goat when both of you get started on me."

"Oh, never mind about that!" Cinnybug reassured him, as she got up from the table and carried the empty cookie plate back to the cabinet. "Cousin Cad told me I need not to worry when I went to see him last week—that I'd own my own home after tonight." She stopped dead, the cookie plate poised. Out in the side-yard, the dog set up a fine yapping, filling the kitchen with it.

"Own my own!" Cinnybug loved to say it. "It's what I've waited for, for twenty-five years." She shoved the plate into the cabinet. "Oh, I know it wasn't your fault, Jellicoe, don't look so hang-dog." She studied him, sitting there slumped in his seat, pucker-faced and red with apology; but she kept on turning away from him until the sight of herself in A'nt Elemere's mirror made her stop, and edge closer to inspect herself.

"What do you think I ought to do about the neck of this dress? It looks so washed-out-looking. What's eating that dog?" She waved her head from side to side, stretching her neck of scraggy tendons and chickeny bones, studying it quite objectively. "Do you think anybody'd mind if I just pinned a little white collar on it? Some people put white on mourning clothes."

"Oh sure, honey, I don't think anybody'd mind."

"You don't!" She said it out of the side of her mouth, because her neck was wound too tight.

"Unhunh." Jellicoe had stopped listening again and roused himself at last to get coffee. Cinny saw him through the mirror.

"Pour me a cup, honey. Oh, for the love of God!" She rushed to the window, where the dog's barking almost drowned her voice. "I can't even see it. John Junior," she yelled, "where are you?" Then she saw the Buick, sleek, high-coloured, and long, parked across the creek. "Lord's love! Whose is *that*?"

Jellicoe took out two cups and went back for saucers and went back for sugar, and then went back again from the table because he'd forgotten the cream. As he poured the coffee, he moaned, "I sure could use a shot!"

Cinnybug realised that the dog had stopped barking, and turned back into the room.

"Well, there won't be any here," she told Jellicoe. "Mary Lee won't allow a drop in the house on account of Amelia finding it. It stops everybody drinking but Amelia. I think I'll copy that collar off of Mary Margaret's dress. She sure does have some nice ideas in clothes when she comes down."

She came and sat down beside Jellicoe and he pushed her coffee towards her. She sat winding her spoon around it, thinking about Mary Margaret, for when she spoke she lowered her voice, but not enough.

"Do you like that foreigner she married?"

"Who?"

"Mary Margaret."

"He isn't a foreigner, is he?"

Not enough because Mary Margaret came slowly on to the porch and heard all she said.

"Well, practically," Cinnybug rejected Julik with a twist of her mouth. "His father was born somewhere out like Poland or Hungary or somewhere. That's about as foreign as you can get to. Of course Mary Margaret's husband was born right here, but I always say you can't make a silk purse out of a sow's ear. I wouldn't call them real Amer'cans, would you?"

Mary Margaret had stopped first because she was too embarrassed at catching them to interrupt, but when

The Kiss of Kin

Cinnybug stopped, she flew at her, scratching the screen-door out of her way.

"A'nt Cinny, never let me hear you make another remark like that about Julik, do you hear me?" Mary Margaret's voice went low and shook with fury and it swamped and froze the two lounging at the table.

Cinny looked at the girl wide-eyed, holding her breath. Then she almost screamed trying to hush her by explaining, "I didn't mean anything by it, Mary Margaret! It's just my way of talking."

Jellicoe nodded wisely, not catching the shock between them: "Sure, Mary Margaret. It's just her way of talking. She didn't mean anything by it," and went on nodding, forgetting to stop.

Mary Margaret didn't take her eyes from Cinnybug.

"Do you know what kind of pain that sort of remark can cause? Do you know how it can twist a person, twist them into a kind of cripple? You wouldn't know what it's like to be hated and alone in this country." She was getting closer to Cinnybug, panting every word, bitterly. "You're the ones who belong some place. You belong! You've got no right to be so cruel!"

Cinnybug fought her away because one of her words had struck home. "Oh sure, we belong!" She began to shriek, "We belong to Mr. Ebenezer B. Crasscopper, don't we, honey, don't we belong to Mr. Ebenezer B. Crasscopper?"

By the time she had finished the tears were running down her face and she was crying loudly, square-mouthed like a child, with her face getting red with effort. Jellicoe jumped up and began to pat her back, thumping out gasps and sobs.

"Help me, Mary Margaret! All this going-on has been too much for her. You know what kind of a day it's been.

You know . . . awe, honey . . . awe, honey . . ." Cinnybug's fists pawed the air in front of her, and her cute shoes drummed the floor, beating time with her sobs.

A'nt Elemere rushed in from the dining-room, like an angry hen.

"Love of the Lamb, what has somebody been doin' to my lil baby?" She fussed as she scooped Cinnybug up and held her thin body jack-knifed in her strapping arms.

"Here you, Mr. Jelly, open that door and let me through." Jellicoe was hovering, making little vague gestures of holding out his arms.

"Can I carry her, A'nt Elemere?"

A'nt Elemere didn't bother to look at him: she was too busy trying to quiet Cinnybug, who was filling the kitchen, like the dog had, with noise. "No, I don't reckon you could, Mister Jelly. You jest stay down here and let me see to her; poor little thing." She went past him, crooning to calm Cinnybug.

Jellicoe turned round to Mary Margaret when they had gone and the kitchen was still again. Mary Margaret stood where she had stopped, inside the door, her face no longer troubled, but numbed by the noise.

"Well, I don't know. I don't know what made Cinny do that. She's real calm most of the time."

"It's today—and tonight to come. That's what's the matter with her." Mary Margaret watched the door; the noise had already stopped and she took a step to follow, to apologise, then shrugged a little and changed her mind.

"You know I'm sorry you heard her say that, Mary Margaret," Jellicoe was explaining sorrowfully. She hardly heard him.

"What in the world's the matter with Cinnybug?" Amelia saved Jellicoe from having to try any more with Mary Margaret by coming into the kitchen so much faster than she usually moved that even he noticed it. When he looked at her, he forgot to answer her question about Cinnybug: her face was grey-white, drained, taut, as if plump, gentle Amelia had seen more than she ought to for her own good.

"What in the world's the matter with you, Amelia? You look like you've seen a ghost!"

Amelia brushed into Mary Margaret, quivered against her shoulder for a second without even noticing her, and flopped down at the table. But when she did speak, she ignored Jellicoe and spoke to her.

"Get me a drink, honey—in the flour bin. Don't for Lord's sake tell your mother it's there, will you."

Mary Margaret rooted out the bottle and blew the flour from it, gathered a shot-glass from the cabinet as she passed, and handed them both to Amelia. "I wouldn't tell her, A'nt Amelia."

Amelia poured a drink and threw it down her throat. She looked at Jellicoe, standing with his mouth ajar, staring at her. "Here, Jelly, you look like you could use one, too." She pushed the bottle and glass at him. "Oh Lord, I just don't know," she began, then took another drink instead.

When Jellicoe had poured a drink, which he was far more interested in, worn out as he was, than Amelia's news, Amelia reached for her bottle, slammed home the cork, and handed it back to Mary Margaret.

"Do you want me to put it back in the flour bin?"

"Sure, honey, put it back." Amelia forgot her again and turned to Jellicoe. "I just don't know what to say," she went on.

Suddenly Mary Margaret, as if she'd been told, understood what had shocked Amelia so.

"You've seen Abraham."

"I've seen Abraham, stretched out in the hammock; just lying there, on the front porch, asleep. It was Abraham, and it wasn't Abraham. The spittin' image; he would be twenty-nine or thirty now at least. Young Abraham, lying asleep in the hammock, just like his father." She was suspicious of Mary Margaret. "How did you know?"

"I know. He came when you were all gone to the grave. I came into the kitchen and there he was, talking to A'nt Elemere."

"Why didn't one or other of you tell us? Why didn't somebody let us know?" Amelia had taken up the empty shot-glass and was twisting it rapidly round and round in her hands. "Oh Lord in heaven, I don't know what to think. What Mary Lee's gonna cut up like I don't know. Well, she'll just have to keep quiet for once. The boy's got a perfect right to be here, the same as the rest of us."

Something about Amelia made Mary Margaret try to question her carefully, asking it into the air, shading her hand at the same time and looking out across the side-yard as if she were drawn to something under the trees. "A'nt Amelia, why would Mother cut up? Why would she cut up over Abraham coming back?" When Amelia didn't answer she went on, "She must have known one of that part of the family would come back to the funeral. What's behind it all? He wants to know."

She turned then at hearing no answer. Amelia's eyes had glazed and she was smiling slightly, neither listening nor answering such questions as that even to herself.

"A'nt Amelia."

"Unhunh?"

"He wants to know."

"Does he? Well, I don't know. Nothing. Just nothing." She laughed and put on sweetness like a coat. "Isn't it nice? Soon as he wakes up somebody had better go talk to him. Make him feel at home."

She struggled up out of her chair.

"I'm going to lie down. This has all been very upsetting."

She stopped as she passed Jellicoe and clutched at his shoulder for support and attention. "Jellicoe, the vault was the coldest place! Did you notice? All those stone platters, and there we all were, kicking just a little too hard to get shovelled on to them. I want to lie beside Charles Truxton." She smiled, and nodded her head. "He was a very fine man."

She was gone, weaving away from the kitchen where people asked so many questions, to lie down alone and doze in the cool and let the liquor take over.

Jellicoe had already started for the kitchen cabinet before the door stopped swinging. "She'll be so potted she won't be able to move by evening. I'm gonna have another shot of her liquor."

He took the bottle back out of the flour bin and blew it. "Keep her from wasting it on herself anyway."

CHAPTER VII

"UNCLE JELLY, oughtn't somebody to tell Mother before she just meets up with Abraham?" Mary Margaret waited, half-poised, half-decided to do it herself, but still ready to be told she needn't bell that cat in the heat.

Jellicoe wasn't worried. "Aw, honey, I been watching this bunch of women scratching too long to take any notice of what gets after 'em most of the time." He stopped to yawn and went on speaking with his words full of air: "This Abraham'll have to take care of himself."

He lounged over and looked out of the back screen-door where he could see Cadwallader still leaning on the gate where the others had left him watching down the road, looking from the back too tired to unbend.

"Hey, Cad," Jellicoe yelled, and the figure began to straighten up. "Come on in here and have a shot. You look all in."

Cadwallader turned slowly and came up the path, his eyes down, his hands clasped together, only looking up at Jellicoe when he reached the steps.

"It's the heat," he told Jellicoe, wiping his face with a clean handkerchief, "I never could stand a sun like this. It makes my head ache."

Cadwallader did look 'all in', from his winter black suit to his Panama hat, for which he'd stopped at the haberdashery in Palmyra and bought a black ribbon, thinking about it for a good long time, and then fitting it on himself in his office. He looked dog-tired with sorrow and the general business of being a cousin at the funeral, expected to be sorry, but not bowed down enough as a cousin not to be able to take over. So he had taken over, for the simple reason that he hadn't been able to see who else in the world would do it but him. In the hot sun, he'd seen to getting the few cars parked, then seen to the undertaker's men having a place to stand, seen to the Company people getting seats in the dining-room; even at the end he had paid the preacher, with the tears ferreting down his thin face and fogging his gold-rimmed glasses so that by that time he could hardly see his change.

"I'm the kind could get sun-stroke—usually inside a cool, green office—room lined with all those dark green tin deed-boxes just about as cool as you can find anywhere; then I have the fan on, too." He bowed his head to come in at the door, although he no longer needed to. It was easy to see where he'd got his permanent stoop, though. Stretched out he would have been six feet five inches tall; not that anyone had ever seen him stretched out, unbowed, strutting down the road, in his life.

Mary Margaret noticed that he had forgotten to wipe under his glasses before he came into the house, and that the tears he had been crying, out over the back gate, still lay damp in the furrows under his eyes. The sight of him made fresh tears spurt suddenly from her own eyes, and she had to turn quickly away and lean on the side of the kitchen cabinet.

"Mary Margaret," Cad was talking to her, but she listened with her back still to him, "you saw one of the finest women you'll ever hope to meet buried today, and don't you forget it. It makes me proud to think that I enjoyed her confidence. Oh, I hope everything tonight goes smooth. It's too hot for everybody to get to picking at each other." Cadwallader began a grin, like a nervous twitch, then stopped, putting himself already in a mood to force everything to go smooth.

Jellicoe, who loved peace as much as Cadwallader, but for his own lazier reasons, caught the warning note and asked, "Is there any reason why everything shouldn't go smooth, Cad?"

Cad sat back in his chair and studied Jellicoe, like he studied clients, calmly and slowly from under his eyebrows; a lawyer look, an ethical, moral, confidential, judicial, client-squirmer of a look he'd picked up at Law School and used, the same as he'd used a Panama hat, ever since.

"Jellicoe, I wouldn't, even if I could, divulge one bit of what's in A'nt Anna Mary's will. I will tell you this much, though. She disposed of her property as she saw fit and proper for all concerned." Then he wasn't bothering to look at Jellicoe any more, just sitting there remembering.

"I remember it like it was yesterday; she come all the way into Palmyra, a day as hot as this. There she sat, all dressed up; she could be a fine-looking woman, you know, when she tried—before she begun to be taken bad all the time. She sat there with her veil blowing nearer and nearer the electric fan. 'Cad, son,' she said—she called everybody son—'I figured out how to deal with my property fair for all and yet not foolish.' Well, I couldn't stand it any more, I said, 'Miss Anna Mary, if you don't git away from that fan you'll be sucked in, veil, hair and all, and you won't have a chance to make a will.'" Cad chuckled and shook his head. "She just said, 'Shucks, Cad, I'm too tough to be sucked up by some little old new-fangled machine.' You know, she went down to the Flora on the corner there as soon as she left me and pushed her way right through all those kids standing around slopping up sodas the way they do, and just give orders for some damn-fool boy waiting behind the counter to bring her what she called a wind-machine. I tell you that soda-jerker hopped to it, though! It's there beside her bed now."

He got up. "I'm going to lie down a little while. Heat of the day, you know. It's best."

He wandered away slowly into the cool of the house. Jellicoe began to complain, gently, before the door had swung shut.

"Ever' time Cadwallader gets upset he'd talk the hind leg off a mule. Other times you can't get a word out of him." Jellicoe went on as he tipped the bottle back into the flour bin, smelling into it before he finally closed it. "Boy, the fumes from the biscuits'll get even to Mary Lee if Amelia don't find someplace better'n this to hide her stuff."

He looked longingly out of the screen-door, and Mary Margaret gave him the push by habit that he seemed always to demand. "Don't you want to go and lie down, too, Uncle Jelly?"

He moved towards the door, grateful. "Yes, honey, I think I will. You know, you don't get much chance, when you work in an office, for a little afternoon nap, especially when you work for a go-getter like Mr. Crasscopper." His apologies were muttered mostly to himself, for he was out of the screen-door and around the porch nearly to the swing by the time he finished.

Alone then, after all the to-ing and fro-ing, Mary Margaret sat at the table, her elbows out and her hand half shading her eyes. The whole house around her seemed sunk in summer sleep; all but the kitchen, where the silence was high-pitched and the sun on the side-porch beat through the dust. Over the table the flies wheeled a little, even though the house had run to a stop for a time. Mary Margaret went on staring at the same space, seeing nothing, sunk in it, not moving her eyes, hardly breathing out enough to disturb the heat around her. Then slowly she put her head down in her arms and tried to sleep, too.

CHAPTER VIII

ABRAHAM, half awake himself, having been caught in the hammock by the sun and roused just enough to make him move, came round the house, taking in everything aimlessly. The old tar barrel used as a rain-barrel; the rocking-chairs on the porches, all wheewhawed but so that you could see what just might be coming down either creek from them; the clumps of striped tiger-lilies; all swam by him, unfamiliar. He felt the ground rise under his feet and, looking up, saw by the stone sundial on the grass mound that it was somewhere near four o'clock.

The quietness of it all besieged him. He felt outcast by it; found the house, with its mothering porches, as forbidding as an empty house; so he walked, without caring or knowing why, back to sit in his own car for a while. He looked back half-way across the creek bridge, and the house seemed small again, as he had first seen it.

Then it was easy to slip back to the disappointment of his first view of it. Nothing. Not a damned monument. Just a clapboard farmhouse with the dun-coloured paint peeling and the trellises sagging under the heavy burden of their ragged old rambler roses. Not a place at all, from right out there across the creek, where you could find yourself kissing a baby-faced stranger just to get the numbness out of her head and your own. But all he said aloud to himself was, "I thought it was gonna be bigger than this," and knew for the first time in years the easy physical urge of wanting to cry.

John Junior, inspecting the Buick, unscrewing whatever he could find loose, thought of course from the centre of his world that Abraham was talking to him.

"It's the biggest car I ever saw from way off. When you git up near it don't look so big."

Abraham slouched over to the car, let himself be drawn into John Junior's questioning, answered one for every dial, and finally to stop them said what John Junior wanted him to, "Do you want to go for a ride?"

"Yeah. I reckon so." John Junior ran round the car and got into the front seat, keeping his enjoyment strictly to himself, getting in and slamming the door with a gesture of half-bored ownership.

He settled himself, and refused to answer Abraham when he asked where he wanted to go, just waited for the car to start.

Abraham turned it back towards the main road the way he had come, beginning to wonder as he drove if it was really true that children took in so much of what was going on. So he realised why he'd taken the trouble to bring John Junior for a car-ride. He looked down beside him and watched the boy as much as he could, driving.

John Junior was slouched back in the wide seat, his legs not touching, but his arm stretched up to where he could let it lie along the window rim, his eyes hooded, trying to look used to it, hiding a high excitement. As they passed a boy in blue jeans and galluses scuffing barefoot along the dirt side of the road, he lifted his arm and waved like the King of England.

The little boy stopped and waved back wildly, his mouth wide.

"Want him to go for a ride?" Abraham asked, slowing down.

"Oh no. He don't care nothin' about cars. He wouldn't want to go, too."

"Friend of yours?" Abraham stepped on the gas.

"I jist know him. His name's Digby or something. I don't know."

They went on down the road past a few houses, more shacks, some high up on the side of the hill as the little creek valley narrowed from time to time almost into a hollow. John Junior took out his nickel-plated harmonica and began to play, trying Abraham to see how far he would go before he'd start the grown-up racket of asking questions and bossing. He sucked air in and out in long wails, making a noise like a piano trying to breathe.

"Can't you play anything?" Abraham said, the noise filling his head.

"This is something."

"Well, don't play it right now. I can't drive." The silence after the harmonica was embarrassing, each of them waiting. Abraham finally asked casually, "Think everybody was surprised to see me?"

So the bossing and the questions started just about together.

"I don't know," John Junior answered, and fingered the harmonica in his pocket.

"Did you hear them say anything?" It was like sticking a foot on to hard ground and finding it was made of mush. It had happened with A'nt Elemere, it had happened with Mary Margaret, and now it was happening with this four-eyed brat. Abraham kept his eyes on the road, taking the turns swinging. "Well, did you?"

"Don't remember nothin' about it. What are you asking me for?" John Junior watched out of the window as the familiar houses, the barns, the fences, the little unpainted Jenny Lind shacks sailed by like new things from a new speed and a new window.

He couldn't contain himself any longer. His joy bubbled

out. "I been down this road about a thousand times," he confided, bragging.

It was Abraham's turn not to answer.

John Junior started to sneak the harmonica out of his pocket again, but Abraham saw the glitter of it out of the corner of his eye.

"Put that goddamned thing away," he said, not bothering to look any more.

"You sure are a dangerous driver," John Junior told him, admiring him at last.

"There's nothing dangerous about driving fast," Abraham said, slowing down. "There's the main road. Want to go back?"

"I don't care," John Junior said, carefully.

Abraham slowed and began to turn.

"There's a real good dog-wagon down the main road a piece if you're thirsty," John Junior told him.

"Make up your mind." Abraham swung the car back round and circled into the main road and down it along the river. He saw for certain that the brat was too fly and too wise and too plain mean to treat the way you'd treat most children; a lot of little chips off an old dumb block, who drew forth meaningless phrases from bachelors; phrases like 'I'll bet you wouldn't take anything for him', over their heads to their parents. Abraham wouldn't have given three cents for John Junior Passmore, even dead.

"A'nt Amelia said it was all the same to her," John Junior told him when they were safe out on the main road.

"Thanks," said Abraham, watching out for the dog-wagon.

"She's high as a kite."

"Where's this dog-wagon of yours?" Abraham was still wary of his little cousin.

The Kiss of Kin

"Down the right, right yonder, where that thar sign is," John Junior pointed, speaking hill-billy self-consciously. "Boy, she's stinking as a billy-goat. Boy!"

"Is that any way to talk about your aunt?" Abraham pulled the car to a stop, swerving it off the road. "Here you are."

"You was thirsty," John Junior pointed out, and disappeared into the dog-wagon ahead of him.

Joe Poppelino's dog-wagon had begun to grow from the seed of his own kitchen table, where, during the 'twenties, he'd started serving a little of his own quite good home-brew, principally because the bottom had dropped out of the coal business and there was no other way for him to make a living for himself. But what Abraham saw, over twenty years later, was a long, thin, low building, with a high narrow false front made of clapboard, on which was painted *JOE'S*, in letters that had once been red. As soon as he bent his way into the door he realised what it was—an old caboose, with home-made tables in between the coupled wooden seats.

That had been added to the front of his shack in 1932, just before Joe, who was as unlucky as he was smart, had been picked up for boot-legging and sent to the penitentiary. When he came out the Eighteenth Amendment had already been repealed for nine months. He went back to the dog-wagon and started serving three-point-two instead of his own home-brew. After he came out of jail he started saving all the human-sized cardboard advertising girls that were sent to him over the years, so that the only colour Abraham could make out in the gloom was a shadow-world of bathing-suited, pert, laughing, dusty girls, some of them in twenty-year-old styles. They were the only women Joe had ever burdened himself with. The only art work he had added was a sign reading

'No use to Ask for Credit' over the dirty, tiny counter.

Abraham slid into one of the dingy caboose seats opposite John Junior. "What do you like to drink?" he asked the boy, and looked around for someone to bring it.

"Joe!" John Junior yelled.

"What'cha want?" came from the door behind the counter.

"Coke."

"O.K." Joe Poppelino, hot and old, worn out by his weight and the summer day, came in through what had once been his own front door. Abraham could only hear him; John Junior, in full view, had made him stop. "John Junior, you got any money?" he called out, bending over the ice-cooler.

"Sure I have. I'm with my cousin."

"Down for the funeral, eh? Ain't it too bad...?" Joe kept on muttering.

"It's Abraham, my cousin Abraham," John Junior called proudly. "He's got a big car."

Joe was uninterested, popping the top off the coke. "I don't want you hanging around here without no money no more, John Junior. I'm gonna tell your A'nt on you. You goddam kids." He knocked on the counter with the bottle, signalling for John Junior to come and get it. "Don't your cousin want anything?"

"Get me a beer." Abraham flipped fifty cents across the table; John Junior grabbed it before it stopped clattering.

"How old are you?" Joe called.

"Twenty-nine. Old enough, mister."

"Oh, excuse me. Now ain't that funny? What do you know about that?" Joe grabbed a bottle of cold beer on his way round the counter, bringing an opener with him in his hurry to see Abraham. John Junior, forgotten for a minute, got his coke and slid back into place with it.

The Kiss of Kin

"Pay the man, buster," Abraham told him. "Can I have a glass?"

"A glass?" Joe was surprised. "Oh, sure. I get used to these kids comin' in here. It ain't good for business, I tell you. Comin' in here."

"Joe's been in the pen. He's scared of getting pinched all the time," John Junior said, sucking at his coke.

"Shut your dirty little mouth." Joe slid back round the counter again and back into his front door.

"What did you say that for? The guy might not like it," Abraham asked the boy.

"Well, he has. It ain't nothing. Everybody around here went to jail for bootlegging. Still do." He hopped up from the table, grabbed a bag of potato-chips from the counter, and scattered them over the table.

"You don't miss much, do you?" Abraham watched him, wondering if the time had come to question him again.

As if he'd caught the scene in his mind that Abraham wanted to force him back to, John Junior began to brag again.

"They can't fool me, that bunch of old, skinny women. I'm gonna git myself some money and I'm gonna leave this old place. I know whur I kin git it, too, I jist gotta whustle." He 'hill-billyed', and wiggled and pushed potato-chips around the table, watching them.

"Do you?" Abraham asked, waiting.

"Sure I do. My dad'll give me anything I want. Anything . . ." He forgot to play with the potato-chips and sat very still, looking at nothing.

"I hate this place and I hate this school. I'm the smartest boy in my room. I have three hundred beer bottles. When I git five hundred I'm gonna sell 'em to Joe and I'm gonna buy me a ticket and I'm gonna do whatever I want to." John Junior finished in a high voice, having recited himself back into confidence again. He sat with his big, spectacled eyes full on Abraham and went on skidding potato-chips.

But Abraham drank his beer slowly, not wanting to ask any more questions.

CHAPTER IX

WHEN Abraham stepped back on to the empty porch, empty because it too was full of sun now, so that the sleepers, knowing the habits of the sun, had not gone there as they would when the evening came, he saw Mary Margaret move her head in her arms, then grow still again. He opened the screen-door softly and went in.

"I can't sleep." She looked at him, drowsy, worried.

"Why is the house so quiet, Mary Margaret?" he asked her, a little disappointed because he had already prepared himself to face the hullabaloo that the news of his arrival would cause.

"They're all asleep."

"They're sleeping off the funeral. It does that to people . . ." then decided against the reminiscence. "What about you? Why can't you sleep?"

"I don't know."

"What's the matter?" he asked, as if he knew, and grinned, so that she wanted to slap his face.

Instead she was rude. "I said I don't know why. Honestly!"

"Don't you?"

"All right. I was afraid to wander around the house because I might meet you. That's why. We might just meet . . ." she ended feebly.

Abraham was laughing at her now, but quietly.

"Don't you care anything about anybody else?" her voice rose at him, "coming down here . . ."

"Nobody who gets in my way in this damned place," he interrupted her. He sat down and leaned his chair back, watching her. "When you want a man it makes you afraid, honey. Maybe you haven't wanted one for a long time. You know, it doesn't have anything to do with whether he hurts his hand, or whether he has talent or . . ."

"Let him alone!" Mary Margaret woke up at last, sat up straight. He caught the movement and tried to help her up from her chair, hugging her; but she found him too heavy on her, disturbing. She twisted away from him and sat back down. "Let me alone, too, Abraham. I can't understand you. Who are you. . . ?"

"I'm your cousin, honey."

"Why are you like this?"

"Like what?"

"Overpowering. I'm a grown woman . . ." she added carefully. ". . . you're acting like a squatter. You've got a perfect right to be here, the same as the rest of us," she explained in an echo of Amelia, and then, suddenly realising whose words she copied, paused. "You don't have to act like that," she trailed off.

When he didn't answer she tried again. "What kind of a place do you come from that you. . . ?"

"Me?" he interrupted her, looking down at her. "A lot of different places. I've worked a long time."

"What doing?"

"I messed around. I got through college washing dishes, so I learned how to wash dishes. Then I got drafted. After the war I went wild-catting. That's where I finally found out I had some talent."

"What kind of talent?" she asked, smiling as if he'd confessed to being a part-time artist, which being of her own world she thought he had.

"My kind, sister." He understood the smile. "I can smell oil when the wind blows, and feel natural gas when

I put my hand on the ground like you can feel Paganini's pulse. But right now I'm curious," he added, and changed the subject impatiently, as he changed his pace up and down in front of the table, making the screened-in kitchen look more like a cage than ever.

"You? I won't ask about you." He looked up her plump arm to her hair and reached out and touched it, tenderly. "You're the kind who gives up things—anything . . ." and almost added 'My mother was like that,' but, angry at his own thought, said instead, violently, "Martyrs herself to anybody who'll have her."

It was all he could do to keep from pulling her hair under his hand. "You've got the rot of this house worse than I have. Boy, oh boy, you just wait for what's coming, you and this house. I'm going to smoke you out."

He looked at her, hating her as much as the rest, so that when Cinnybug burst in from the dining-room at her most hysterically social, they might have been strangers for all she could tell. She rushed up to Abraham and kissed at him, missing and smacking the air behind his ear. Then she held him out at arm's length, like she would have a little boy, only she had to look up, not down, at him, jabbering all the time.

"Well, if it isn't Abraham, after all these years! Just think! I'm your A'nt Cinnybug. Why, we'd of been right here to welcome you, one of the family like you are, if it hadn't of been that we were up to the vault when you came. Well, let me have a look at you! Isn't this nice, Mary Margaret?"

She turned to Mary Margaret, twittering, "I'll declare I had NO idea he was coming! I wish it could have been at a better time, but never mind, it's an ill wind . . ."

Even Cinnybug ran down at last. She was silent, staring, smiling uncertainly from one to the other of them, wondering when somebody would say something, then adding feebly:

"Here we all are."

"Who told you Abraham was here, A'nt Cinnybug?"

The question was enough to set her off again happily. "A'nt Elemere told me, honey, why, tired as I was I just had to get right up and come right down here to welcome you. After all it isn't as though you were a real stranger even if none of us did know you, blood's thicker'n water. Not that we wouldn't, of course, you look just like your father, a chip off the old block. I reckon ever'body tells you that. I'll declare it's been a long time. How's your father? Why didn't he come?"

"I was the one told to come."

Cinnybug went cold all of a sudden, and she could not hide it. "Told?"

"A Mr. Cadwallader Williams wired me two days ago."

"The very day. Did he? Well I never! Cousin Cad!" Politeness and panic raced in her voice. "Well, you just make yourself right at home and I'll try and find some of the others."

She ran out through the dining-room and stood at the hall door, bawling.

"Amelia! Mary Lee! Jellicoe, where are you?"

Mary Lee could be heard coming nearer, trying coldly to shut her up.

"What are you yelling around for, Cinnybug, today of all days? If you don't have any respect for your own mother . . ."

For once Cinnybug interrupted her.

"Listen here, Mary Lee, do you know who's in there?"

"Who?"

"Abraham, that's who!"

The Kiss of Kin

Mary Margaret tried not to look at him, but there he was, listening calmly, taking it all in.

Cinnybug went on, "So you'd better just dry up that kind of talk and get in there and behave to him. . . ."

Mary Lee sounded bitter, more bitter than even Mary Margaret ever heard her. "You tell me why I should after . . ."

"I'll tell you all right! It's not the father, it's the son. Cad sent for him to come. It means he's been remembered!"

"Remembered!" They threw the word at each other like stones. "I might have known. Remembered! Huh! Mighty fine words swallowed to come back, I'll bet! Well, a little promise of money sure does work wonders. . . ."

Mary Lee swept into the kitchen, followed by Cinnybug, straight up to Abraham, while Mary Margaret tried to make it all right by saying:

"Mother, this is Abraham."

Mary Lee stuck out her long hand, blue-backed and lumpy.

"Glad to see you, son. It's a bad time. We should have met in easier circumstances. . . ."

But Abraham was not behaving as he ought. He dropped her hand, and left her high and dry with even her small effort.

"What words have I got to swallow?"

Mary Lee was far too surprised to do anything but meet him on his own kind of battleground. After all, you listened, but you didn't stand up and brag about it.

"What do you mean? Do you mean to tell me you stood there and listened to what I was saying? I never heard such downright brass in all my born days . . ."

Abraham's anger mounted with hers. "O.K. Just tell me what you meant."

The Kiss of Kin

"You ought to know what I meant. If you were too young to remember you musta been told. Your father walked through that door one day a long time ago, leaving a lot of fine words about what he thought of us all behind him." She stopped explaining to Abraham and began to accuse him, throwing her hands outward with disgust. "Oh, mighty fine words, scorning everything, talking big; telling us all just what he thought of us. What we had to sit here and listen to was more than your grandmother could stand." Then gradually her attack centred on his presence in the room. "He said he'd never come back, but I notice he wasn't too highfalutin to send you when there was any chance of things being shared out. You'll have to forgive me if I talk in a way that isn't very welcoming, but we're all upset today, and I reckon we say what we think easier."

Abraham mused, forgetting her for a minute.

"It's beginning to clear, what I came here for."

"What's beginning to clear? I should think it was pretty simple, what you came here for. Money."

"A picture."

Mary Lee understood them completely, at once, and took Abraham for as big a fool as she'd taken his father.

"Abey asked you to get something. He always was a sentimental old fool." She flopped a hand outward again, giving him the whole house. "Well, carry away all the junk you like. There's nothing here but a bunch of junk."

Cinnybug couldn't stand it. She complained quickly, whining, "Now, Mary Lee, don't you talk like that! You know Mother promised me the early 'mercan sideboard, why, I had my dining-room designed for it twenty-five years ago just so some day I'd have room."

Mary Lee didn't bother to look at her.

"It's just some junk he wants. Sentimental junk." She pushed open the screen-door.

"Now excuse me. Any other time there'd be a little more to your welcome. But today we're all a little bit on edge."

She went out, letting the door plonk behind her; she sat down straight, folding her arms and her lips, but letting her legs hang limp in the rush-seated rocker, and began to creak gently back and forth, forgetting them, watching out beyond the few trees where the land bent down to the creek.

Cinnybug edged closer to Abraham, too pleased almost to ask, "Do you mean you don't want any money?"

"I didn't say that."

Cinnybug kept from crying. She just said, "Oh," and it was like a little sigh.

Abraham looked out of the door to where he could see Mary Lee's legs bending and straightening in the rhythm of her rocking.

"He always hated being called Abey. He never allowed me to be called by it."

Mary Lee's voice sounded farther away than just the porch. "Mary Margaret, come here. I want a word with you."

"Yes, Mother."

Abraham held her back by both arms, almost hugging her, ignoring Cinnybug, and said, "Don't go if you don't want to. She only wants to bite your arm."

Cinny was surprised enough to forget about the money for a minute. "What kind of talk is that?"

Amelia, hearing voices, quickened her careful navigation of the dining-room and burst in on them, swaying a little but determined at last to carry off a decent welcome. "Hello, Abraham!" She waved her arm like a lone cheer-leader. "Welcome to our city!"

Abraham smiled. "Hello, A'nt Amelia."

"You knew me!" Amelia shook her head at him in some surprise.

"I knew you the minute you bent over me in the hammock."

"So you weren't asleep."

"No."

"Just playing possum." She smiled again, less certainly.

"It would have scared you if I'd said anything. You looked all in."

Amelia, the smile not quite gone, just forgotten, began to sidle towards the kitchen cabinet. "Has Mary Lee seen you yet?" she asked over her shoulder.

"Yes."

"Where is she?"

"She's right outside the door." Abraham had recognised Amelia's crab-wise sneaking and he warned, grinning with an understanding which made her fat face coy with complicity. She had arrived at the kitchen cabinet, but at his look she took her hand from the handle of the flour bin, turned, and flopped down at the table. Mary Lee called out again, this time with tight impatience, "Mary Margaret, come here at once!"

"Yes, ma'am." She almost ran out of the door before Abraham could stop her.

He exchanged glances with Amelia and she grunted a little laugh. "Well, the pore youngin's only twenty-seven years old."

Abraham sat down beside her. They both ignored Cinny, who was fidgeting in the shade of the sink, listening.

"I don't get it," he said. "Mary Lee seems to run things, but she's not even a daughter."

"No," Amelia told him, shrugging it all away from her, "it just slipped to her. You know how it is. Cinnybug there was too young. I was just married and only coming back for little stretches. Mother had to have somebody here with her. Your father and mother were here for a little while, right after the war. Then they left." She was already getting tired of explaining, finding excuses. "John went out to Persia in oil. We've been getting letters for a long time. Then he come home and left his youngin here. His wife died out there. Never met her. There just wasn't anybody else. Mary Margaret's father spends most all of his time in one hospital or another. So Mary Lee got to taking over. It was the best thing. This is a big house to run."

Abraham glanced again at the thin legs, bending and straightening as Mary Lee rocked, talking to Mary Margaret in a voice that for once no one else could hear. "That woman would drive me nuts in a week."

Amelia said, following his eye, "Don't pay any attention to her. Mary Lee's all right. It's just her way. Nobody else . . ." She shrugged.

"How long have you been back?" Abraham forced her then to look straight at him and she began to defend herself.

"My husband died! Seven years ago now. I came back for a few weeks to get over things. Buried him here, but not in the vault because they all said that was only for the immediate family. Get over things." She clung to the phrase, trying to remember what it was she had started to tell him. "There wasn't much of a place for me to go. Not with a youngin. Not with Mary Armstrong. So I been here ever since." Then she remembered what it was, waked up a little and really looked at Abraham, proudly.

"I got plans for opening a little antique shop. Not a big one, just a little one, with little tiny things in it." She made a small space in the air with her fingers and looked at it lovingly. "I just love nice things. It's never happened yet, but someday it will. Charles Truxton was a very fine man, and he was as good to me as he could be."

What had been for so long a habit-phrase suddenly sounded defensive. "He left me seven hundred dollars. I was going to start a little store."

"But you never did."

"No. I never did. Charles was very good to me. No. Never did."

"And now you haven't got the seven hundred dollars."

But Amelia had slipped completely away from him. She got up and brushed past him, saying as impersonally as if she had touched a stranger in the street, "Excuse me," and then passed on forgetting both the person and the touch. She wandered away, her footsteps sounding out through the house.

CHAPTER X

WHEN Cinnybug realised she was alone with Abraham, she began to babble across him as she fluttered to the door where she hoped Jellicoe would be dozing on the porch.

"My, my, I must find Jellicoe and tell him you're here. Jelly!" Her voice pierced at the curtain of sleep around him, and he turned in the hammock. "Come around on this side! Come on!" She heard a grunt from him in answer. "We've got a big surprise for you!" She peeked round the screen and saw him beginning to pick himself up like a heavy load out of the old hammock made from bed-springs, covered with a matted-together mattress and scraps of rug.

"Jellicoe always lays around there out of the sun when he can shoo the dog off. He dudn't get much time for naps," she explained over her shoulder to Abraham.

Then, when Jellicoe hadn't come, she jumped to the next thing she could think of.

"Have you had anything to eat?"

"Yes, I have." There was another silence. "Some potato-chips," Abraham added, and wished he hadn't.

"Oh," Cinnybug sighed.

Jellicoe was at the door, inside it, smothering a yawn, then holding out his hand and saying the wrong thing.

"Hi, boy. I heard you'd turned up!"

"Like the bad penny. Yes." Abraham shook his hand.

Catching Cinnybug's eye, Jellicoe stopped the beginnings of a grin and started to apologise. "Now you know I didn't mean anything like that, Abe."

"Nobody ever calls me that." But even though Abraham

tried to soften his answer, Cinnybug gasped with embarrassment, and Jellicoe was afraid to say anything more. They stood there, the three of them, watching each other until Cinnybug couldn't stand the silence any longer. She giggled, and the sound tailed off into words, "It's been a long time."

"A'nt Cinny . . ." Abraham started to speak, but Cinny interrupted him with another giggle, because he was standing nearly a foot over her and calling her 'A'nt'.

"What were the words my father should have swallowed?"

Cinnybug tried to pass it off as something silly. "Oh, I don't know what Mary Lee was talking about. She gets things on her mind. You know!"

"You mean you do."

"Honest, I don't, do I, Jellicoe?"

"Why didn't I ask Amelia?"

"Oh, she won't tell you anything!"

"So there is something to tell!"

Mary Lee, hearing it all, called out to Cinnybug before she could make any more trouble than she had already.

"Cinny, come out here."

Cinnybug fled, stumbling out of the door. "—Sure, Mary Lee, sure, I'm coming."

Mary Lee only said, "Now sit down here and see how long you can keep your damn-fool mouth shut." Then there was silence on the porch. Abraham turned towards it to go out after them, and even Jellicoe knew that somehow he had better slow this man down before he'd started something that wouldn't be finished until the migraines clamped and the doors all slammed and the voices were pitched almost high enough to make the dog howl.

"What do you do for a living, Abe?" Then he stopped short, remembering too late about the name.

The Kiss of Kin

But Abraham was turned to him, looking as happy as somebody about to start off on a trip.

"I make things."

"Oh yeah. Things."

"Trouble. I make trouble." Abraham's desire to laugh was so great he had to turn his back on Jellicoe. He added weakly, trying to control it, "What is it around here . . . ?"

Jellicoe looked all round, not understanding, even at the ceiling, where he saw only the same old kitchen paper and the wheeling flies. "What you looking for?" he asked politely.

But when he looked down again Abraham was staring at him so that he felt caught in a joke.

"The bomb. Before the blast there's always a silence. Just like this. Everybody waiting . . ."

"Oh, you were Over There! I couldn't go. I . . ."

There was a thunderous knock on the screen-door to the back gate. It made both the men wheel round. A boy of about fourteen, grown out of his jeans and high-coloured shirt in all directions, was standing peering through the door into the familiar house, which for the day had become a strange and almost sacred place. He remembered to say "Telegram", holding the yellow envelope up beside his head.

Jellicoe opened the door and reached for it. "Hi, Tig, what is it?" he said, worried.

"Condolences," the boy told him, now taking in the stranger. "Oh." Jellicoe fished in his pocket and found a dime. Tig pocketed it and ran off, wondering all the way what you ought to say to people in grief, whether you ought to say thank you, thanks a lot, or something like that.

Mary Lee had come in from the porch at the sound of

the boy's voice; she grabbed the telegram out of Jellicoe's hand and began to rip it open in little fast jerks. "Here, give the thing to me. I'm the only one capable of reading it today. Taking it in." She was silent for a minute, reading for all of them. "Oh."

"What's it say?" Cinnybug had to ask before Mary Lee was ready to tell.

Mary Lee wiggled her shoulder impatiently to shut her up, and went on reading. Then she was ready to tell.

"It's from John," she began and she was right back to her funeral weight. "He says he just got our telegram. Listen. He says here, 'To the Passmores, prostrated by news stop my condolences in time of deepest grief stop sorry too far to come to funeral stop love to John Junior signed John'." She held the telegram still where she'd read it, poised, but no longer looking at it.

Cinnybug began to cry. "Poor John. He loved his mother. Isn't it just awful he can't be with us today? Mother would have wanted him here. Mother!"

Jellicoe found his handkerchief somewhere and began to dab at Cinny's face. "Never mind, honey, never mind." He put his arm around her shoulders. "Never mind. Everything's going to be all right!"

But Cinny found his arm too heavy; after all, she'd been so nervous all day she'd wanted to scream at the weight of her black dress and her shoulder straps; the thought made her voice rise, made her forget tears. "I just can't stand any more. I just can't."

Then she let out, as if they all didn't know and have it weighing on their minds too, what was really upsetting her; what was bolted down in her mind as solid as a rail to a tie while everything else flittered through.

"Abraham!" like a cry, "what do you do for a living?"

"I drill oil-wells."

Cinnybug felt suddenly sick with joy. "You mean you've got money?"

"A lot of money."

She was over the edge into hysteria and she began to babble, laughing, with the telegram tears still falling down her face.

"So you really did just come down here to get a picture! He really did, Jelly, he did just come to . . ."

Mary Lee crushed the telegram in her hand and forced it into her pocket. "Shut up, Cinny!"

Cinnybug was completely silent.

A'nt Elemere, pushing her way through the group still standing at the door as they'd gathered to hear the telegram, muttered, " 'Scuse me," and tiptoed over to the stove.

Mary Lee watched her go. "A'nt Elemere, what are you doing pussyfooting around in here right now?"

A'nt Elemere got out a big spoon and began to stir the beans again, not bothering to turn round but answering, "I'm taking my green-beans offn your shoulders, Miss Mary Lee."

Mary Lee had found something besides a piece of paper to take her painful spite. "You're getting sassier every day."

But A'nt Elemere wouldn't crush like telegrams, or daughters, or flittery cousins. "If I wudn't here, you'd be calling me a sassy nigger," she said complacently. "Seem like they don't nobody but coloured people use that word no more."

Abraham ignored the rest and went over and leaned on the sink beside A'nt Elemere, watching her potter around the stove while he ignored the others.

"A'nt Elemere, what did my father say when he left here?"

Her face went blank of every personal thing about her. There was just coloured woman left, but not A'nt Elemere. "I disremember. He said so much I disremember it all."

"You're a liar." But he couldn't change her.

"Yessir."

"You didn't hate them. They told me so."

He couldn't even blackmail her.

"No, sir."

He admitted defeat.

"But you're not going to tell me."

"No, sir."

"Why not?"

A'nt Elemere drew herself up from her bosom, her elbows stuck out while she felt for her knot of brown-black fuzzy hair, straightening it, and, in the process, putting a large hairpin in her mouth and talking through it as if she'd given up paying any attention to anything he might have to say to her.

"Good servants dudn't repeat what they done pick up from time to time," as if any damn fool ought to know that.

"A'nt Elemere, you're an old fraud."

She stuck the hairpin back, wilfully misunderstanding him and both of them knowing it.

"No, I ain't, Mr. Abraham. I ain't never stole no money in all my life, Lord Jesus listen to him!" She clucked on to herself, grinning.

Mary Lee marched past Cinnybug and Jellicoe and stood stock still in the middle of the room, ready and impatient to 'get it over with', 'have it out once and for all'.

"If you've got anything on your mind, young man, I wish you'd come right out with it instead of talking all this foolishness. You're just like your father. It's just him coming out in you. He always was grinning around like he knew some joke. What are you sniffing around for anyway? If you want to know anything, whyn't you ask your father?"

"He's dead."

A'nt Elemere dropped her spoon on to the floor with a clatter and hid her face in her hands.

Cinnybug talked.

"Oh, how awful! We'd of come if we'd of known! Nobody told us!"

Mary Lee was furious, not about the death but about the conventions of the death. "Do you mean to tell me that that woman didn't even bother to tell us when one of Miss Anna Mary's own sons had passed away?"

"He didn't want her to."

Mary Lee snorted. "You mean he was downright ashamed to talk about us!"

"He died laughing at you."

Mary Lee went white, sick-looking, but before she could answer, Cadwallader, innocent and sad, came in from the dining-room to do his duty by Abraham, still pulling down his shirt-cuffs after putting his coat back on.

"Well, if it isn't young Abraham!"

He was delighted, reading nothing in their faces.

"You'd know him anywhere, now, wouldn't you? Welcome home, my boy. I'm sorry I wasn't here when you came, but . . ."

Mary Lee interrupted.

"Cad, what on earth do you mean by not telling us that Abraham was coming?"

Cadwallader began to apologise long before he decided what to say.

"Well, Mary Lee, I didn't know for certain. You know

The Kiss of Kin

how it is. All the arrangements to be made, I reckon it just slipped my mind."

"Slipped your mind!"

Cadwallader's apology faltered at her disgust. Then he went on:

"Well, I didn't think you all ought to have more to think about on a day like this. I just didn't want there to be any more trouble than there need to be."

He pleaded for peace, turning to Abraham, "You understand, son. All that there was to do, and you a close relation they hadn't seen in so long."

He went closer and touched Abraham's shoulder, forgetting even Mary Lee.

"One of the last things your grandmother said to me was: 'Son' (she called everybody son), she said, 'Son, you get that boy back down here,' she said, 'I'm sick and tired of all this trouble,' she said, 'I'm an old woman'; but she was a handsome woman, just as handsome as you could imagine, almost up to her passing. 'Get him home,' she said, 'I'd like to see the boy. If I can't, I'd like him to know I don't bear no grudge.'"

Cinnybug had been trying to ask, finally interrupting, "How did you know where he was, Cousin Cad?"

"We been in touch. After Abraham died . . ."

Mary Lee stepped closer to him and he dropped his hand from Abraham's shoulder.

"You knew? You knew all the time?"

"Well, Mary Lee, I'd sworn to Miss Anna Mary not to tell you all. She was more than strong-minded, as you all know. She said, sitting right in that big overstuffed chair in the living-room she liked so much, 'Cad,' she said, 'I can't stand them youngins talking about Abraham again after all these years. Let him rest in peace.' Then what else she said is still private."

The Kiss of Kin

He'd always known that sooner or later he'd have to deal with Mary Lee and he was determined she wouldn't get him riled.

"Cadwallader, you're one of the purest-bred damn fools I ever heard tell of." Her voice was still low. That was one thing. "Do you mean to tell me you let that old woman wrap you around her little finger so you kept everything from us?"

"Now don't be like that, Mary Lee. It's all long past. I don't see any sense in stirring up a lot of old trouble and neither did Miss Anna Mary."

It was the wrong time for Julik to come in, all set to be sociable after his nap.

"Did somebody call me?"

"No." Mary Lee was so off-hand that Julik, half asleep, couldn't yet hear the sting of that small word.

He smiled, explaining, "I thought I heard somebody call me. I do that sometimes. I . . ."

Mary Lee's mouth went awry with scorn.

"Call you! Hunh! I couldn't pronounce your name!"

Julik stepped back and looked square at her, surprised at first; then he turned away and almost ran out of the screen-door to the side-yard.

Abraham had hardly seen it all. He was intent on keeping Cadwallader to the point. As soon as the door slammed, he attacked him.

"What old trouble? Tell me, what old trouble?"

Cadwallader tried to head him off the point in the past, just as he had Mary Lee, standing between them and making half-finished calming pats towards each of them in turn, missing them both with his useless-looking scrubbed hands.

"Now, son, you better forget all that. It's a long time ago and I'm sure everybody's sorry. You know, one time everybody lets their temper run away with them, and then there's trouble none of us want. She wouldn't have wanted it all brought up again."

Mary Margaret came in from the porch and touched her mother's arm gently to draw her attention.

"Mother," she whispered.

"What?" Mary Lee shook her hand away and ignored the girl, interrupting at a time when she couldn't be bothered with her.

But Mary Margaret was so still in the room, after the strength of men talking and the rising of the argument, that she created a silence, drew their eyes to her and even her remark, as intimate as a secret, spun round the room and included them all.

"What did you say to Julik?" she asked her mother.

"I didn't say anything to him. I hardly even spoke to him."

"He's out there and he won't talk at all. He's white, like somebody had slapped him. What did you say to him, Mother?"

Her question hardened, and Mary Lee jerked herself out of her grasp.

"Mary Margaret, how dare you use that tone of voice with me?"

Amelia, swinging open the dining-room door, caught the two of them for a second, frozen in a pantomime on the edge of quarrelling.

"Oh, oh, what's all the shootin' about?"

Mary Lee shut her up. "You keep out of this."

But the question had unfrozen them, toppled them into fighting.

"Tell me what you did!" Mary Margaret forgot her calm pitch and let out a woman song.

"I didn't do a damn thing," Mary Lee sang with her.

"You did. You turned your viciousness on to Julik. He's the one person in the world I'd protect from you. Let him alone, do you hear me? Do you hear me? I won't have you hurting him. Julik is worth more than all of you put together!"

Mary Lee looked round the kitchen at the silent watchers.

"Are you all going to just stand there and let her talk to me like that?"

Amelia laughed with a snort: "We been waiting for somebody to for twenty-five years."

Mary Lee spoke then, remembering where she was and who were all ears, with an icy dignity, thrown on as quickly as a coat.

"You'd talk to me like that! Talk to your own mother like that in front of the kind of people I despise. After all I've been through; you ought to be ashamed!"

It was the loathing in her look that made Mary Margaret realise something she oughtn't and weaken with sorrow at it, so she tried to make amends.

"Oh, Mother, I didn't mean to. Oh, Mother, I'm sorry if I hurt you." She reached a hand to touch her, but Mary Lee twisted away, too breathless with anger to do much more than whisper, "Don't put your hands all over me. Hurt me! You couldn't. You just disgust me."

John Junior bolted in through the screen-door like a sudden gust of wind, blinded by his own tears, howling as he breathed. He felt a way through the kitchen full of grown-up legs to A'nt Elemere and clutched her apron, bowing his head as if he'd been whipped. She took him by the shoulders, gently this time, and spoke as lovingly as she held him: "For the love of the Lamb, little sweetheart, what's the matter?"

John Junior's face was streaked with dirt and tears and

snot. His glasses were filthy from rubbing it into a mess of shame and sorrow with his tight grimy fist.

What the matter was all came out, with just time to sob between the shoals of trouble. "A'nt Elemere, my grandmaw's dead and Mary Armstrong says I won't be able to live here any more and she says my socks always stink and nobody will play with me and nobody likes me!"

She took off his small gold-rimmed spectacles and started to clean them on her apron-corner behind his back as he buried his head again deep against her thick legs. Mary Lee couldn't stand it any longer. She grabbed John Junior, lifted him by the arms, and thrust him in front of her on to the table, screaming over his sobs to stop him.

"Shut up! Shut up! Shut up! John Junior, what's the matter with you? Stop that noise and tell me! Tell me, do you hear? If you yell like that you'll be sick and I'll give you castor oil! Castor oil! I'll give you castor oil!"

Then she was quiet, shaking, and so was John Junior, blind-eyed and new-born-looking without his glasses, staring at her.

CHAPTER XI

AMELIA thought she heard somebody on the sunporch, but wasn't sure. "Lord God Almighty, it's hot," she said, not caring whether they heard her or not. She stripped off her shoes and stockings and flung herself down across the bed. Nobody answered her, so she forgot, lying down, and sighed to herself. Far away in the downstairs hall the clock whirred and chimed six times. A little evening breeze from the hillside, almost within reach of the window, caught the long net curtain, then her hair. She turned her cooled head as if it had been stroked, already half asleep.

Julik knocked lightly, then, getting no answer, louder, and stuck his head in at the door. The room he saw was like the one that he and Mary Margaret had slept in, so like it that for a minute he didn't realise he was in the wrong room. The same white carved-wood bedroom fireplace with gas logs; the same brown and chrome criss-crossed linoleum, with slippery woven mats flung over it in patches; the same net lace curtains, still with a jaunty air as if a long time ago they had been 'the very thing'; but even before he saw Amelia on the bed, Julik knew it was not the right room.

It was the dresser that told him. It was made of ivory wood trimmed with thin gilt lines, and to see it there was like discovering a frilly parasol blown down a warehouse street. It was covered with a lace mat under glass, and on the glass, like toy ships on a model ocean, were Amelia's belongings; her pin-tray of imitation ivory, her pincushion made like a hard red heart, her snapshots, birthday cards and Valentines, and a few 'studies' of the family, egg-shaped on squares of white paper, some in silver frames, and some stuck into the mirror, and long since curling outwards with age. But among the whole collection there was not a single one that could possibly have been Charles Truxton Edwards. Amelia had spilled powder sometime across the surface. It covered the objects with a thin film-like age. The powder-box leaned crazily against the pin-tray it matched, celluloid with a dirty puff on a stick thrown across it. It looked so neglected, so personal, that Julik backed out again as if he'd happened on a woman dressing and didn't want to be caught.

But Amelia struggled up, frightened, and called, "Who is it?" It brought him back into the room.

"Oh, it's you, Mr. Rosen! Lord, there don't nobody knock around here. Come on in."

He still stood, half in, half out of the door. "I was just looking for Mary." He saw her bent and bunioned feet, and for a second felt sorry for the poor woman, whose name he couldn't remember, lying propped on one elbow on the bed.

"Haven't seen her, son. Come on in." Amelia helped herself up, and fumbled her feet into her shoes.

"Well, if you want me to," he hesitated, his injury coming back. He sat down in the rocking-chair by the fireplace, but kept it from rocking, watching her.

"Lordy, it's hot," she said, twisting round so that she could see him.

"Not so bad as it was," he told her carefully; then, launching his hurt, belligerently, "I guess I'm not very welcome around here."

Amelia was surprised. Then she remembered. "Lordy, son, you don't want to go taking every little thing so seriously." She snorted. "You won't last long around this boarding-house if you do. Mary Lee was just teasing you." She was sure he didn't hear her. "What do you care, anyway, smart as you are?" When he still didn't answer she gave him up and lay down again, talking this time to herself, but letting him hear if he wanted to.

"I remember . . . Lord, it doesn't seem more than yesterday. I started getting myself all dressed up to go out with my best beau. They thought they'd play a little joke on me, so Mary Lee offered to frizz my hair. She liked a little bit of fun in those days. Boy, did she frizz it! I went out of here looking like a singed chicken's ass. Abraham . . . that's the boy down there's father . . . he didn't think it was so funny." She was silent for a minute, wandering off on her own dreamy track, then she turned her head to Julik again. "That was the day my beau bought me flowers for the first time . . . store-bought flowers. He sure did put on the dog!"

Julik's chair creaked as he leaned forward to interrupt, "She wasn't kidding me!"

"That was just before he took me to Tennessee. Have you ever been to Tennessee?" She gazed at him through the brass pattern of the bed-end.

"I hardly been outa New York. I been working too hard since I was fourteen . . ."

"Tennessee's so pretty, right up near the North Carolina border. We had the cutest little house. Wait a minute, son, I'll show you a picture." She got up and walked carefully round him, sliding her untied shoes. "It's not very good. It doesn't show the lovely slope down at the front." She blew powder from a snapshot in one of the silver frames and handed it to him, pushing it between his fingers as she hung on to the chair-back and nearly made him rock with her weight.

He glanced at it politely, seeing a little white clapboard cottage, with a front porch, nothing to rave about, just like a million others even in places like New Jersey that he knew about. He was so annoyed with the woman that he nearly told her so. But when Amelia, gazing at the picture over his shoulder as intently as if she'd never seen it before, sighed and said, "My goodness, it was a pretty little old place," he didn't answer at once, but leaned across her and set it back, carefully, on the dresser.

Amelia looked down at him as if she'd just discovered he was there at all, and smiled. "Mr. Rosen, how would you like a little drink?" she asked him.

"I'm thirty-four years old and I never been farther than Jersey City when I met Mary," he answered.

"Isn't she the sweetest little old thing? Now I'm going to pep you up with a little drink."

"You people down here . . ." he began, and stopped.

"Just a little shot to perk us up." Amelia carefully hoisted a bottle out of the closet and poured a drink into a water glass.

"Thanks," he said, when she handed it to him. He thought of asking for water in it and then decided against it. Behind him, Amelia tipped the bottle up to her lips, then went back to lie down.

"Aren't you having one?" Julik turned the glass in his hand.

"You go ahead," she said, lying down again. "Gwan! It's good for you. The little things of life." She began to shout, "To hear her go on, you'd think it was a damn crime for a person to want a little peace and quiet once in a while!"

"Who, Mary?" he asked, trying to follow.

"Mary Lee!" Amelia flung herself back on the bed and was quiet. "What's the matter with a little fun once in a while?"

"I never had much time for it," he told her. "You wouldn't know. You've never had to teach. I hate it, all that time wasted." He tipped his drink back and finished it. "Maybe it's over."

Amelia watched him lazily. "Mr. Rosen, you're not a bad-looking man if you'd put a little meat on your bones."

"My mama was always trying. So does Mary. It's worry. I can't get enough sleep." Amelia let her eyes go past him and stop, staring at the vacancy of the ceiling.

"Charles Truxton ate like a horse," she interrupted, and went on staring, now out of the window to where she could nearly touch the trees on the hill. "When Charles Truxton was home . . . but then, he travelled so much . . ."

"You travelled much?" she asked politely, remembering for a second that she had company. Julik looked at her, smiling there, slouched across the bed, and realised at last that she had been drinking.

"Charles Truxton covered the three states—weeks on end." She laughed. "Mary Lee's sure horsing around today. Lord, she gets my goat sometimes, horse-arsing around. She's just born to organise trouble. . . ."

"Well, thanks for the drink," Julik said. "I'd better find Mary. . . ."

"Aw, don't go off like that!" Amelia jumped up from the bed. "You let that youngin alone." She came over between Julik and the door, suddenly as mad as a wet hen.

Julik started round her. "Look, lady, lay off!"

But she caught him by the arm. "Now you just sit down, Mr. Rosen. We're going to be friends." She pushed him back towards the chair. "What's your hurry, drinking my liquor?"

"You people . . ."

"What about us people?" She stood over him.

"Nothing."

She sat back down, forgetting she'd pushed him, as soft as she'd been hard the minute before, swaying and dreaming again.

"I've always wanted to go to New York. It's one of my secret ambitions. Tell me all about New York."

Julik tried. "You've got to live there. Get caught up in it. It's tough—tougher than you people down here know. First thing I remember" (he started to rock at last) "was an eight-storey tenement with only one toilet."

She had lain down again and closed her eyes.

"Nobody ever flushed it," he called to her. "It stank up the whole hall."

But she didn't open her eyes.

"When my dad died, Mama moved in with my grandparents. Things were terrible, too many of us, not enough to eat—terrible. I was ashamed; you people have no idea. All those dark red lampshades with fringe, how could I explain what they meant? The smell of grease right down the hall when you were coming home, and everybody screaming so you couldn't think. Then my grandfather would step in and shut everybody up. He was the boss, always the boss. I was his favourite. At Passach he would choose me. You see, I was the youngest. And if he had a nickel to spare, even a dime..." Julik was rocking slowly, caught up in his story, telling it carefully to himself, taking for granted that the woman on the bed would listen.

"We were more cultured than most of the others; little bit better people, you know? My grandfather started me on my music. Mama said it was crazy, but he was the boss. He's still alive, still believes in me. He says to me, You start out good anyway in music. At least you're a Jew...."

Amelia rearranged her back on the bed without opening her eyes.

The Kiss of Kin

"He isn't afraid of talking about the soul, things like that, you know?"

She sat up politely. "Why, Mr. Rosen, I didn't know you were Jewsh! Well, I'll declare . . ."

"Didn't you?" he grinned at her self-conscious pronunciation of the word. "Say Jew," he ordered her.

She was as solemn as she could be and still be half-drunk, and slopped all over the bed quilt. "Lordy, you've got a chip on your shoulder all right!"

"I'm just telling you the facts. When you grow up with it . . ."

She interrupted, not hearing him. "Mary Lee said you were foreign, but she didn't say Jewish."

"My grandfather doesn't speak a word of English. Yiddish, Hebrew, Russian. He's a smart man."

"Well, what do you know? I reckon you think we're just plain dumb. All those languages." Amelia made her eyes wide to seem interested. "Would you like another little drink?"

"No, thanks," Julik got up again. "Now if you can spare me, I'm going downstairs."

"We've been around here so long we just don't bother . . ." She didn't get up.

"Yeah, you stuck yourselves in, you people." He was at the door, "Thanks for the drink, anyway."

As he closed the door behind him, Amelia shrugged and got up. "Oh, Mr. Rosen, you bite like a dawg," she said happily to the mirror, patting her marcell. Then, as she listened more carefully for footsteps, she found the bottle again.

CHAPTER XII

UP in the attic, still hot with the last of the sun, though it was almost evening and the rest of the house had grown cool, Mary Lee squatted on her thin haunches and tore paper. Before her on the floor stood boxes, piles of old magazines, and a book or two, swollen twice its size with having things stuck between the pages.

It took two long rips, with her hands turning as if she were wringing out clothes, to divide one of the thick letters, already grown yellow, hardly legible for age, but something, like all the rest spread around the floor, that had belonged to Miss Anna Mary which she'd put away a long time ago and forgotten or not. A pile of playing cards, big ones with bicycles on the back, were puffed out with damp and age so that they stacked drunkenly, spilling away from each other. Mary Lee was adding them in little groups to the pile of waste, letting them slide slowly out of her hand, like some card-trick into a hat. But she didn't notice where they fell; she was listening to the voices of the children, playing way down below her on the side-porch, waiting for supper to begin.

She couldn't hear what they were saying, so she gave a little jerk to her shoulders to tear her eyes from their blank staring and set to work again among the papers. The pulp books of ghost stories, the Church of God pamphlets, an advertisement of a Half Moon, a pile of unused Sunday School good-conduct cards, suddenly a peacock feather, long and loose among the trash, all but its bright eye worn to brown fringe, a poster of a revival meeting showing a young man with his hair slicked back like Wallace Reed, and his hands in doubtful attitude across his chest and clasped together, SUNDAY Jesus Means Business. MONDAY The Skeleton Key to the Golden Gates. TUESDAY Die in the Canona Valley: RISE IN CHRIST. Mary Lee threw them all on the pile, which had grown so high that it tumbled backwards under one of the brass beds.

She ripped the string from around a pile of letters, settled herself more easily on the floor and let them drop loose into her spread-out lap.

"Mary Lee? Mary Leeye?" Cinnybug called out in a big half-whisper from the floor below, and almost as soon as she had called, her head appeared above the floor of the attic.

"Oh, there you are."

Mary Lee didn't answer. She had begun to sort the letters, ripping each one through the middle and throwing it on the waste paper.

Cinny looked around over her shoulder. "I'll declare, it's still all I can make myself do to come up here. It sure is scary, isn't it, Mary Lee?"

"It is for those that scare," said Mary Lee, throwing another letter on the pile. Cinny settled herself on a pile of quilts on the bed.

"What are you doing, Mary Lee? Hadn't you better wait . . . ?"

"Oh, it's just some junk of your mother's. No use to keep it around littering up the place. Just a lot of junk she had laying around here for years and wouldn't let anybody lay hands on."

"Don't you think we all . . ."

Mary Lee sucked her teeth at the litter on the floor.

"There's nothing here hardly worth the burning." She was scornful. "I'll declare, the things she kept! A lot of trashy books and some letters from people I never even heard of, sister this, and brother that." She tore at another letter and threw it on the rest.

"What's that?" Cinny's eye caught on to a bit of brightness as quickly as a magpie and she jumped down from the bed to pick it up. But it was only a Christmas card, bright blue, with the Wise Men of the East going towards a little sand-coloured village with the Star of Bethlehem hanging over it like a bright electric light. Inside there was a message, *God Bless Sister Anna Mary on Christmas 1929, Brother Beedie* in careful bad writing.

"Hunh," said Cinny, "I remember that year—that was when he got religion right after he came out of jail. Mother's had him laying around here ever since. What in the world would she of kept a thing like that for?"

"Don't ask me." Mary Lee had destroyed the packet of letters, and she picked up another one.

"Mother thought they were all just fine till she sneaked in one day on Brother Beedie's girl, only nine years old, stealing her Florida water and sprinkling it all over her little bare jezebel." Cinnybug giggled. "I thought it was some little bit of cloth," she explained, throwing the card back on the trash heap.

"What did you want to do? Sew yourself up some little old tacky collar? I'll declare you're as tacky as your mother." Mary Lee was already half-way through the next packet of letters.

Cinny watched the pile grow larger. "Mary Lee, it dudn't seem right on the very day, getting into all her things."

"It's about time, from what we heard this afternoon. You never can tell what your mother kept back from us all in her old age. I'm not going in there tonight without making sure, I'll tell you that right now."

"Well, I just thought it didn't seem right."

The Kiss of Kin

"You better be glad somebody around here is doing a little thinking. Are you going to help, or are you going back downstairs? Here, hand me that basket, and start helping to pile some of this junk in it."

Cinnybug bent over the pile, holding the basket close beside her. She made a little squeal of pleasure. "Look here, Mary Lee. Here's a picture of me when I was little. Mother musta kept it special, not in the album, I mean."

But when she drew it out Mary Lee had torn it in two, neatly, through the middle.

"Well, I'll declare!" Mary Lee held up a newspaper clipping, then put it down secretly into her lap and started to read, bending over it. Cinny craned over.

"What's that?"

"Nothing."

"Whyn't you throw it away, then?"

Mary Lee made a 'shhhut' noise to stop Cinny interrupting her. She went on reading.

Mary Lee Elecky, the daughter of Mr. and Mrs. Samuel J. Elecky, was married on Saturday at twelve o'clock at the First Methodist Church South to Mr. Nathaniel Longridge, of Palmyra, West Virginia. The church, banked with seasonal rambler roses, made a beautiful setting for the radiant bride, who was dressed in white voile, with a white lace veil which is a family heirloom. Miss Elecky was educated at Montmorency High School where she was valedictorian of her class. Her higher education took place at Miss Mimpson's Seminary. She has been for the past two years president of the Younger Women's Suffrage League, and is prominent in local theatricals. Miss Elecky's father has been for the past eighteen years associated with the Intercounty Fuel and Power Company. Mrs. Elecky, the former Miss Virginia Myers, is of a prominent local family. Mr. Longridge is associated with the Century Colliery Company.

The Kiss of Kin

He was educated at the State University where he took a degree of Bachelor of Arts. He is the son of Geoffrey Longridge, of Palmyra, a distant relative of Col. Longridge of Civil War fame.

Whatever more there had been to the clipping had been torn away.

"Gosh, what'd she want to keep all that kind of stuff for?" Cinnybug got back at Mary Lee for tearing her picture.

"Dammit, Cinny, gwan downstairs and let me alone. I came up here with a headache and I don't want to be bothered with you." Mary Lee looked at the clipping again, then tore it slowly across and threw it on the pile with the rest.

Cinnybug went off down the stairs, not daring to look behind her until she was past the first-floor landing. She found Amelia, still stretched out on her bed barefooted, watching the hillside out of the window.

"Mary Lee's up there into all Mother's things. I don't think . . ."

"Aw, let her alone. Nothing up there but a bunch of junk. Anything important Mother would of put in the bank vault." She turned her back on Cinny, heaved over in the bed, and closed her eyes.

Cinny slumped down beside her, just as Mary Armstrong slipped into the sewing-room next door. The whirr of the sewing-machine made both the women jump. Cinny ran to the door.

Mary Armstrong was pounding away at the fancy wrought-iron treadle with both her small feet, making the needle go so fast she couldn't see it dive and lift out of the table, sending the wheel skidding round so that the crossbars ran in and out of each other under her fist.

Amelia roused herself from the bed and called, "Mary Armstrong, I thought I told you to leave that machine alone." She said it so weakly that Mary Armstrong couldn't hear her through the throddle of the machine.

"It's not good for it to run without any material under the needle," Cinny yelled, explaining. Mary Armstrong took her feet off the treadle.

"Hell, she knows that." Amelia lay back down on the bed. The sewing-machine had run down and was silent.

"Now run on out, honey, I'm trying to have a little rest," she murmured to Cinny as if she were a child, too.

As Cinnybug started down the big front stairs, she heard the whirr of the sewing-machine, faintly behind her, starting up again. Amelia had evidently got past caring, because it went on and on until she was out of earshot.

She pranced out of the front door on to the main porch. Jellicoe and Cadwallader sat side by side in high rockers, watching the empty road.

"What are you two boys up to?" Cinnybug interrupted.

"Nothing, honey; setting and thinkin'." Jellicoe grinned at her but it changed into a yawn.

"Or sometimes you jest set!" hooted Cinny, catching on. She plopped down among the chintz pillows of the swing.

Nobody said anything. Cadwallader hadn't looked round or stopped the slight rhythm of his rocking.

But when Cinny started to swing lightly he said:

"For Lord's sake, Cinny, honey, can't you keep that swing quiet?"

"It needs a little oil." She looked up at the big hooks in the roof where the chains rubbed, and then sat very still, waiting for supper.

"Miss Mary Lee? Miss Mary Lee?" A'nt Elemere pulled her bulk up the stairs by the rails, calling all the time.

High above her she heard Mary Lee's voice.

"What do you want?"

Looking up, she saw her peering over the attic banisters down the stair well.

"Is it all right if we eat in the kitchen? Can't nobody but Solly put that dine-room table up again and he ain't coming back till morning."

"Well, I reckon we'll have to." Mary Lee was impatient. "Reckon we'll have to do everything in the kitchen if it comes to that. Oh, Lord." Her head disappeared, and A'nt Elemere saw just her fingers, tracing up the banisters back to the attic.

"Well, supper's ready, then," she announced.

Cinnybug heard her from the porch and jumped up.

"Come on, boys, let's eat this dirty little bite!"

"Come on, Cad, or we'll wait for you like one hog waits for another," called Jellicoe back to Cadwallader, who hadn't even moved in his chair.

CHAPTER XIII

BY the time supper was over, the twilight had almost ended, and in the near darkness the space between the house, the trees, the corn cribs, the chicken-coops, had lengthened like the shadows. A'nt Elemere, shaking the table-cloth out in great swinging flaps over the edge of the side-porch, could just barely see John Junior, running down among the trees near the creek. She turned back into the kitchen, folding the big cloth, took it back into the dining-room and stowed it into the early American sideboard.

As she was finishing the last of the dishes, Mary Lee came in from the dining-room, and switched on the electric light as she passed, making the twilight outside the window go completely dark, and signalling the start of the evening. The light sawed a path through it out of the windows and the screen-door, all the way down towards the coops, but petered out before it got there. John Junior's form disappeared.

"What you want to sit around here in the dark for, A'nt Elemere, I don't know. You'll end up breaking all the dishes."

Since A'nt Elemere's sitting around had consisted of washing-up after nine people, she didn't answer; she just thought.

Mary Lee drummed on the screen, looking out, then turned.

"Let me know when you're finished, so we can start."

A'nt Elemere went on drying up, stacking the dishes on to the big table.

"I'm almost washed-up, Miss Mary Lee. Almost."

The Kiss of Kin

Mary Lee bent down, searching through the kitchen cabinet.

"Where's the molasses can?"

"I ain't seen it."

"Everything gets all wheewhawed on a day like this. Everything gets out of place." She found the can, hidden behind the cereal boxes where it didn't belong, jerked it out and slammed the door.

"Lordy, I'm tired," she murmured as she went out of the screen-door. "I wish we'd start."

Cinny held open the dining-room door and looked in, but Mary Lee had disappeared, and there was only A'nt Elemere, drying the dishes in the harsh kitchen light.

"Where's Miss Mary Lee?"

A'nt Elemere motioned out of the window with her head.

"Out feeding the chickens."

Cinny came in.

"She's late."

"She reckoned Effie'd do it, but Effie went home."

A'nt Elemere had begun to put the dishes away, stomping back and forth across the floor so that Cinny had to get out of her way.

"She musta thought it was Sunday."

"Who?"

"Effie musta."

Cinny fidgeted around the room and then said quietly:

"Are you almost finished? We oughta get started."

"Almost." She went on putting away the dishes, neither slower nor faster than she had before.

Cinny ran out of the screen-door on to the side-porch, then seemed to forget why she was in such a hurry, for she sat down in the rocker, pulling it behind her to where she could get a good view of the kitchen. John Junior nearly walked over her, coming up to the door, carrying a large preserving jar.

"John Junior, come right back here and say excuse me," Cinny called after him.

John Junior backed up, still intent on the jar, and said, "Excuse me, A'nt Cinny," neither knowing nor caring if he'd passed in front of his aunt, or stepped on her foot. He flopped down at the kitchen table, put the jar in front of him and rested his chin on the table so that he could stare straight into it.

"What you got in there?" A'nt Elemere poked her head down near his.

"Lightning bugs."

"Oh." She straightened up and began to gather another stack of dishes to take to the cabinet.

"Ain't it time for you to go to bed, John Junior?"

He paid no attention, but after a while said:

"A'nt Elemere."

"Hunh?"

"Why can't you say dead when somebody is dead?" He straightened up and watched her.

"Why do you have to say gone before or passed over or gone to glory when it's a person?"

A'nt Elemere went on working, not looking at him.

"I don't know, honey. You just do 'cause the Bible says there ain't no such thing as dyin'." She knew before she'd finished that that hadn't been the right answer.

"You mean grandmaw might come back and ha'nt us?" John Junior was scared, but enjoying it.

"No, honey, no." She began to stack the glasses. "You dies in the flesh but you doan die in the spirit." She was still for a minute. "You pass over," she said, coming back to the table. John Junior was so still she thought she'd finished with him.

Then he said, "Over what?"

"Oh, the pearly gates. I don't know." She was annoyed. "You quit askin' so many questions. It just ain't polite to say dead when it's a person. That's why. And if you ain't got good manners Miss Mary Lee'll tan your hide." She stumbled and one of the glasses flew out of her hand.

"Now look what you went and made me do!"

"I did not." He forgot about humans and went back to watching his bugs, with his head down, his eyes against the jar.

"A'nt Elemere."

"Hunh?" She was sweeping up the glass, holding the dust-pan with her foot.

"Do you know what I'm gonna do?" He didn't wait for her to answer.

"I'm gonna take these lightning bugs and I'm gonna go out in the woods, and when I see something that needs looking at, if I have these lightning bugs with me in the bottle then I won't need a flashlight, I'll just use these lightning bugs. . . ."

"Unhunh," said A'nt Elemere, wiping away the last of the damp on the drain-board and wringing out the rag.

"If you squash a lightning bug the tail just keeps on being light for a minute. . . ."

A'nt Elemere filled the top of the coffee-pot with fresh grounds.

"It's dead in front, but it isn't dead at the back. . . ."

Mary Lee came in quickly from the back path.

"John Junior, why aren't you in bed?"

He had begun to unfold himself from the chair when he heard her voice. "Yes, ma'am." He began to mooch towards the dining-room.

She followed him out, speeding him up as she came nearer.

"You get a good wash. I'm going to come up there and look to see." She went out after him, swinging the door.

Cinny pushed open the screen-door and stood in it.

"Oh, I wish we'd go on and start." Then she noticed A'nt Elemere setting the coffee on the stove.

"What are you putting that on for?"

"Jest some coffee." A'nt Elemere lit the gas and it gulped into flame. She set the pot over it. "I'm gonna keep some coffee on all through."

Cinnybug's face curled with the intensity of trying to make A'nt Elemere understand. "A'nt Elemere, you can't stay! We've got legal matters to discuss!"

"Then I better stay," A'nt Elemere said shortly. She turned the gas down low.

Up in Miss Anna Mary's room, in the dark red plush chair across the fireplace from the matching rocker, where he'd sat a thousand times listening to Miss Anna Mary, Cadwallader sat in the mottled dark and waited for something to happen.

He'd laid the brief-case across his knees, and he patted it from time to time with the tips of his fingers, feeling to make sure he hadn't forgotten it. Nothing happened in the darkened room. The gas-fire, seeping through tiny symmetric holes in the imitation logs, made a slight hum, and shot patterns of light round the walls. Through the door, half-opened because Cadwallader had been afraid to shut it finally, afraid to throw himself full tilt after what he sought by shutting himself away from anything human, he could sense the emptiness of the hall. He almost got up and went downstairs to start, then he seemed to realise that the first movement out of the chair, out of the room, down to the others, wouldn't end till the fur was flying, so he shrank back a little into the chair, and waited.

He tried to feel something, tried to catch a sense of something, but his own senses never left him: the sound he heard was still the hiss of the fire, and the cold fingering his neck only the night draught through the half-opened door in from the empty hall. But there was nothing, nothing he couldn't feel before any job he had to do where he knew there'd be trouble; nothing special, no feeling of added strength that he was doing Miss Anna Mary's work. The very emptiness of the room was proof enough that Mr. Cadwallader Williams, and that the whole lot downstairs besides, were going to have to shut their own doors and start their own fights, for there was no nice feeling of surety in the air that he could tell himself came from Miss Anna Mary Passmore. She was gone; gone as if she'd been blown out; dead.

Cadwallader stirred in his chair, hearing the clock whirr, getting ready to strike. He'd had his last bit of help from Miss Anna Mary, and he knew it. Having failed with her, after sitting with his nose perked for half an hour hoping and fearing for something to happen which he wouldn't be able to explain, he eased himself awkwardly forward, put his head down on his hand, his arm resting on his knee, and began a short, embarrassed, lonely prayer. Then he reached on down and switched out the fire, so that Mary Lee wouldn't find him wasting gas in high summer, and got up to go on downstairs and get the whole thing over with.

Mary Lee heard the clock strike from the dining-room as she went through to the kitchen.

"Where's Cadwallader? Why don't we start?" Then she saw what A'nt Elemere was up to.

"What are you putting that on for? We just had some."

A'nt Elemere was heavily calm. "You all'll be needing

a lot more before you're finished tonight. I wouldn't feel right if I didn't stay and look after you."

Mary Lee was exasperated. "But we don't need you any more after you've finished with the washing-up!"

"Neb' mind." A'nt Elemere settled herself. "I know them legal talks. They doesn't end up until ever' fuss all the way back to birth done been dragged out and shook up, and ever'body's teeth is in ever'body else's neck." She never would have sat down in front of Mary Lee and Cinnybug, but she did the next best thing. She backed up and sat her bottom against the sink, managing to look immovable.

Mary Lee tried to humour her the best she knew how.

"A'nt Elemere, that's all foolishness! Now go on to bed."

A'nt Elemere didn't seem to hear her. She was rolling her head from side to side.

"Deeds! Ever time you starts unlocking that deed box, out come a knock-down-carry-out fight."

"What can we do with you? You're as stubborn as a mule." Mary Lee began to pace up and down in front of her.

A'nt Elemere remained calm; pleased with herself.

"Naw. A little sense jest rubbed off on me from Miss Anna Mary, that's all."

Mary Lee stopped.

"A'nt Elemere, you're going on upstairs out of the way or we're going to have our meeting in the front room."

A'nt Elemere heaved up straight. "No'm." She was too positive even for Mary Lee. "I'm stayin' right down here. You all'll all get to scrappin' and get so riled up there won't none of you be fit to drive a car without somepin' hot to drink." She played her final card. "There ain't a table big enough with the dine-room table down for all you all to get your elbows on anyway."

Jellicoe stuck his head in at the door.

"'Bout ready to start?"

"Can't you wait to carve up the estate a little bit longer?" Mary Lee slammed out to the side-porch and sat down in the rocker.

Jellicoe came into the kitchen.

"She sure is a mean woman," he almost whispered to Cinny.

But Mary Lee heard him and she called out:

"I just pride myself on speaking the truth. If you can't stand it, it's no skin off my nose."

Abraham, leaning against a tree with his legs outstretched, heard her high voice carry clearly across the dark yard. It was the first clear word he'd heard since he'd sat down to smoke, watching the house with all its windows lit, like a huge doll's house, the edges of it fuzzy dark against the night sky. He went on watching, relaxed against the tree, and took a long drag from his cigarette. Mary Lee, seeing the light move far away, took it for granted it was a lightning bug.

Inside the house, Cinny turned, almost tearfully, to Jellicoe.

"A'nt Elemere won't go on to bed. Oh, A'nt Elemere, I wish you would." She began to whine. "You're just getting Miss Mary Lee all upset."

"Unhunh." As if doing that were nothing to be worked up about!

Even Cinnybug saw then it was no use arguing.

Abraham lit another cigarette from the first, and went on watching the house, taking it in, what there was to notice in the dark: lights going out in far rooms as more of them came down to the kitchen, figures passing casually near the kitchen doors so as to be ready, to be on the dot, but not eager. He could hear the solid creaking of Mary

The Kiss of Kin

Lee's rocker, a high sound that was Cinnybug's voice in the kitchen. But he stayed where he was, in the dark, waiting by the tree.

Cinnybug leaned against the cabinet, looking out into the yard. She held her hand out, vaguely, towards Jellicoe.

"Gimme a cigarette, honey."

He felt around in his pocket and brought out a packet.

"Here." He lit them both and for a minute they stared, side by side, blowing smoke through the screen into the light behind Mary Lee's head.

"Jellicoe."

"Unhunh?"

"Do you think we could go to a new rug in the dining-room? I always did plan to have one when the early 'mercan sideboard came to me."

Jellicoe took a deep drag and sighed it out in a line through the screen.

"Well, honey, you know it'll be your money, so you gwan do whatever you want to."

But the sigh had ruined Cinny's dream. She snapped:

"Oh, now, Jellicoe, don't be that way! You never do seem to take any notice of the house."

She opened the screen-door to the back path and started out.

"After all, you been working a long time to keep the interest paid up. So, in a way, the home'll be part yours." The door slammed behind her and she sat down on the steps.

"Twenty-five years," said Jellicoe, following her out. He sat down beside her, waiting for it all to begin. Even Cinnybug was quiet at last.

Mary Margaret laid underclothes out on the bed in neat piles, while Julik sat and watched her.

"Mary, we only got two hours and twenty minutes until train time," he reminded her. "When do we start?"

She laid Julik's pyjamas out and began to fold them carefully. "There's no use being impatient, Julie. It won't be long."

She began to lay his toilet articles across a canvas bag; he leaned forward and took away a nose syringe and began to blow at his nose as he slouched back in the chair.

When he put it back, he noticed something funny about the clothes.

"Hey, Mary, what's the idea? You've separated everything."

"It's easier on the train." She laid her dressing-gown across the bottom of the smaller suitcase. "It gives us each a case to take into the dressing-room when we go to bed."

"Oh."

"Last time I waited nearly an hour for my tooth-brush."

"Well, I'm sorry, Mary." Julik was offended. "Do you think I like all this stuff? If I didn't take it you'd be the first to squawk."

She went on packing, hardly hearing his voice. "After all," he went on, trying to force kindness from her, "you're always belly-aching when I don't follow my doctor's orders, aren't you?"

She heard something that sounded like a question, so she murmured, "What did you say, Julie?"

"After all, you wouldn't get much sleep yourself if I didn't."

The truth of that was so much a part of their relationship that, not having heard what else he said, Mary Margaret wondered why he'd bothered to say it.

"Well, isn't it about time we went down?" He went to

the door and held it open for her. "These people make me feel like a pin in a bowling alley."

"Look, Julie, it won't be long. I wanted to come by myself, but you insisted."

"I only wanted to come to protect your interests, Mary. You need it with this bunch of vultures." He went ahead of her down the hall.

"The sooner we get out of here the better, while we've still got our hair," he smiled back at her. She started down the steps after him without answering.

CHAPTER XIV

AMELIA almost staggered into the kitchen. "Let's get started. Where is everybody?"

Mary Lee was just getting herself out of the rocker when she heard Amelia. She came into the room. A'nt Elemere was answering Amelia's question with a grin. "They're all at points around the kitchen, all watchin' and waitin' for somebody else to sit down first."

Amelia took possession of a chair by falling into it. "Well, I'm sittin' down!"

"You're practically lying down." Mary Lee passed close to the chair and gave Amelia a look of disgust. She neither noticed nor heard.

Abraham threw away the last of his cigarette and came into the kitchen when he saw the others, through the window, beginning to gather around the table.

"Hello, Mr. Abraham Passmore!" Amelia made an arc with her arm, half-waving.

"Hello, A'nt Amelia, when do we start?"

"Pretty soon." She grinned. "Old home week. You just wait." Then she laughed. "Wait till we get to shootin'!" She stopped, began to dream. "Mother wouldn't forget me. I'm going to have a little store."

Abraham sat down beside her and patted her arm. "With another seven hundred dollars?"

She turned on him, jerking away so hard she nearly lost her balance. "You leave him alone! Charles Truxton was a fine man. Everybody can't be practical."

A'nt Elemere, watching the signs, interrupted them. "Want some more coffee, Mr. Abraham?"

Julik and Mary Margaret came in from the dining-room and stood near the door, both wondering where they should sit. Amelia was staring at the ceiling. "I like to lie in bed and dance. Pretend I'm dancing."

A'nt Elemere handed the cup to Abraham. "You like sugar, I noticed." She set the bowl down in front of him.

"I like to dance until I'm almost asleep, so's I can carry it over into a dream—" Amelia looked sadly at Abraham, wondering—"but I never do!"

Julik was liking the smell of the new coffee, but he was still smarting from being told he'd taken too long in the toilet. "Mary, do you think there might be enough coffee for me to have a cup, or do they serve it to outsiders?" he asked.

Mary Margaret saw the mood and wondered what new thing had caused it. She tried, by habit, to make amends. "Julie, I'd have gotten you some, only I knew you never drank it at night. Do you think you ought to?"

"Oh, for God's sake stop fussing, Mary." He looked around, explaining. "She's all the time trying to nurse me."

She found a cup and motioned him to a chair opposite Abraham. She was too busy handing him the coffee to see that everyone was watching her.

Julik caught Abraham's eye and it made him speak, casually. "What kind of work do you do, Mr. Passmore?"

"I'm an oil man."

"Oh." Julik was careful. "I'm afraid I don't know much about that world." He tried to make it sound apologetic enough to make up for his lack of interest. Mary Margaret reached across and handed him the sugar.

"You prefer being a straw man."

"I don't get you." He was aware of the eyes of everyone in the room fastened on him, watching him being waited on by their Mary Margaret as if she was coloured.

"Have a good look. You want I should take off my clothes?" He tried to pass it off as a joke, but nobody smiled.

The door opened and Cadwallader came in quickly, with a business-like stride, as if the whole thing depended in the end on the sure pace of his feet at the beginning. The whole room was as still as a holding of breath, watching him come up to the table. As if by plan, they'd left the centre chair empty, and Cadwallader, taking the place for granted, leaned over it and placed his brief-case on the table, upright, so that the little brass lock and the gilt initials, C.J.W., were all that they could see.

"Clear these cups off the table," Mary Lee whispered stridently to A'nt Elemere. Then she sat down on the other side of Amelia, to keep an eye on her.

"Well, well, well! Here we all are!" Cadwallader looked round the table, checking them off. "Abraham, Amelia, Mary Lee." He looked round the other side of the table. "Mary Margaret. Now let's see. Where's Cinnybug?"

She opened the door, almost ran in, and sat down opposite Cadwallader, patting the chair beside her for Jellicoe. "Here we all are!" Cinnybug beamed round the table, but no one had heard her.

"I wouldn't smoke if I was you, Cinny, not during the reading." Cadwallader looked at her over the brief-case, trying to make rules as he went along so that the familiar kitchen would take on, by omission, an atmosphere of law and discipline he felt it sadly needed to curb them all. Cinny put out her cigarette with a great air of dignity, but Cad knew he hadn't quite made his point.

When the screen-door swung to behind Cinny and Jellicoe, a tall man detached himself from the tree-trunk by the gate. All that could be seen of him in the dark was

The Kiss of Kin

the shadow of a bony, white face, his long, gnarled hands out in the air in front of his stomach, clutching his hat, and the faint outline of his shirt, light against his dark suit.

He was so scared they'd notice him that he tiptoed even so far from the house, opened the back gate slowly and sneaked up the path, waiting in the grass beside it, then moving a little forward through the dark, until he stood edged up against the rain-barrel, watching through the back door where he could see A'nt Elemere, back leaning against the sink, with her arms folded.

Inside, Cadwallader began to fumble with the lock of the brief-case.

"Now I'm sure you all want this to go off as smooth as I do," he heard him say. The tiny lock clicked back and Cadwallader locked it again in his hand, removed the little key, and put it in his watch pocket.

The man by the rain-barrel leaned forward, keeping out of the light, and cupped his hand to his ear, clutching his hat to his stomach with the other hand.

Slowly Cadwallader drew out the thick, white, folded document. Then he laid it in front of him, carefully, straight on the table.

"If you have any questions, save them until the end. Take your turns. I'm sure Miss Anna Mary wanted more than anything else for you to be satisfied as far as her duty could see to do it."

He started to pick the will up again, but only patted it as he remembered something. "She said to me, just before she died, she said, 'Cad, I hate to think of my family all splitting up and living in rented houses and not having any background when I'm gone.'"

Amelia forgot and lit a cigarette. Nobody noticed. Cadwallader's voice went on:

"You've got to see to it that there don't anything like

this happen. She had youall in mind. She certainly had you in mind."

Mary Lee moved in her seat. "Go on, Cad, stop running for office."

He turned away from the will altogether and began to rummage through his brief-case, making a quiet shuffling of papers like a mouse.

Amelia threw her cigarette down.

"For heaven's sake, Cad, go on!"

Cadwallader looked at her sternly. "Amelia, don't get impatient. These things all take time. I'm looking for a second paper I ought to have ready just in case any of you want to refer to it. You can't be too careful at a time like this."

Amelia blew smoke in his face.

"Amelia, I thought I said we ought not to smoke during the reading. I don't think it's right."

"What in the world difference it makes . . ."

"Oh, for God's sake, put it out, Amelia! Anything . . ." Mary Lee told her.

"Go ON, Cad!" Cinnybug echoed in a high whine.

It made him look up and arrested his arm in mid-air.

"Now, Cinnybug, don't you start getting het up."

Jellicoe half whispered:

"Cinny, honey, you know you ought . . ."

"Oh, hush up, Jellicoe." Cinny's eyes were fastened on Cadwallader's arm. He moved it down into the brief-case again. "Here it is. It's the old will your father left." He brought out another thick, rich fold of paper, this one richer because of the faint parchment colour of age. He began to unfold it and look carefully through it.

"Now I think we might go through this if anybody's forgotten it." He looked up over the will.

"Have any of you forgotten it?"

"No!" Mary Lee almost screamed before she could stop herself.

Cadwallader went right on slowly inquiring round the circle of faces.

"Perfectly clear in your minds?"

"Perfectly clear," said Amelia. He happened to look at her just at the end of the question.

He reached forward and buried the old will carefully among his papers, zipped the brief-case closed, put it down on the floor beside his chair, and picked up Miss Anna Mary's will again.

He held it up in one hand and began to pass his other hand gently across it.

"There's something I think I ought to tell you before I read you this."

Mary Lee shifted in her chair; it creaked like a groan.

"Miss Anna Mary wrote her own will in her own words. She brought it down to me to get it witnessed, and see if it was legal."

Slowly, as he talked, he let the will fall back on to the table again, but no one could stop him, no one could make him move faster. It was as if they were being charmed into a slow movement of their own, against their will.

"Of course it was legal! Miss Anna Mary knew as much about the law as I ever did . . . anyway about deeds and claims and wills and all the civil side. Rightoways! Just take rightoways. She was smart as a Philadelphia lawyer about rightoways."

He went right on, conjuring up Miss Anna Mary in his apologetic voice. Mary Margaret, sitting watching her hands folded in her lap as objectively as if they were little animals that might spring up and run away, couldn't shake herself free of Cadwallader's slow memory. There was not a sound round the table.

"Now this will has some things in it besides property. Some mighty fine things in it. Some sensible talk from the grave."

Mary Lee sat up and started to comment, then seemed to change her mind.

"Property isn't the only thing a woman can leave behind her. Not by long shot. She came in, and she said, 'Cad, I've made my will.' Just like that."

He looked round the table to confound them, but not a single one of them was looking up towards him any more.

"I'd been trying to get her to for years on and off, but she said she was in Jesus' hands and she'd be darned if she could do any better. You know how she was."

No one answered or agreed or looked up, not even when he grew quieter and less nostalgic and said:

"But something happened that changed her mind. So she came down ... walked over from her usual trip to the bank one morning with the document in her pocket-book. But it was legal."

He caressed the long paper again.

"Air-tight!" He gave it a little slap and threw it open. "Here it is."

He adjusted his glasses and began to read, looking hard at the paper as if he didn't almost know it by heart, rehearsing this hour in his troubled dreams.

"*My name is Anna Mary Passmore.*"

Mary Lee gave a tiny snort. "What an ignorant way to start!"

Amelia waved her hand at her to shut her up.

But she was too late. Cadwallader had heard her and stopped reading.

"It's good enough. It's legal in spirit. Law isn't always a bunch of fancy words. Law is something better'n that. It's a spirchal contract too. The spirit meaning more than the words." Cadwallader was already lost in his own philosophy, so he came of his own accord back to the will.

"Now pay attention. . . . *Anna Mary Passmore. I am saner than any one of the people I come up against so I reckon this means I am of sound mind. All right. This is my will. Not my wish. My will.*"

There was not a sound in the room. All of their eyes were poised on Cadwallader and the words.

"*All you youngins have felt me crack the whip before so you know what I mean by the word will. I always swore I would write down what I wanted done with all this property. I didn't care.*"

Cinny couldn't stand it any longer. She began to wail, turning to Jellicoe.

"Jelly, this isn't a will at all! It isn't in any of the right words!"

"Now wait a minute," Cadwallader interrupted. "You just be patient and polite, Cinny, it's like your mother talking . . ."

"Long-winded!" Amelia said it, but she whispered it so low that no one but Abraham heard her.

Cadwallader looked at Cinny for what he thought was long enough to quiet her, then he began to read again.

"*This morning, this being the tenth of September, 1945, I have heard some news about Abraham at last which has changed my mind . . .*"

He felt, rather than saw, an interruption from Abraham, who had jerked his head up and was staring at him.

"Yes, Abraham, that's what it was. That's how long it took us to find out about young Abe. She possibly couldn't wait to hear any longer, so she had me try and track him down. Well, son, it was too late. Your dad had been dead on eight years. I always figured she must of sat right down in there in her room and written this within a few minutes after hearing. You'd think from that it didn't affect her much, but she was that kind of a woman, always took action, some kind of action, when things got too much for her. That's just the kind of thing she would of done."

He found his place on the paper again. Abraham was still.

"*My boy Abraham is dead. If I could of imagined in all my born days that I never was going to lay eyes on Abraham or hear from him again, I don't think I could of stood it. But there comes times when you have to face up to things. This morning I've got to face up to the fact that I won't see Abraham until I get to the other side. Ignorance makes you foolish; makes you stand for too much some times. I waited too long for that boy of mine to write to me. He went away mad. He had a reason for that. All of you youngins who are listening to this will of mine for the last time know in your hearts that he had a good reason. But he stayed mad too long. I can't do anything about that now, but what I can do I'm going to. This is the last time there's any chance of my family splitting up and running off to where you can't get back when you're in trouble and need a roof over your head. If I can't do anything else, I can provide that for you. So I want things divided up in the following way.*"

There was a stir round the table that made Cadwallader's voice falter as he read, but when he looked up to meet the wave of voices, no one said a word. He went on reading.

"*This is to insure that none of you turn your back on any of the others, for I've had enough back-stabbing and picking at to last us all many a lifetime, and I'm sick of it. If you won't love each other any other way, I'll tie up this land and property so you'll be legally bound to have some respect for each other anyway. I'll tie your hands and make you learn to love each other.*"

Abraham interrupted, as if by some pressure he could stand Cadwallader's voice no longer:

"Go back. I've got to find out something. Go back to the beginning."

"For heaven's sake, the damn thing's wordy enough without him having to say it twice." Mary Lee started to pluck at Abraham's sleeve to make him sit down.

"Abraham, son, take your turn." Cadwallader begged. "I've got to read it right through. It's the law. It's the way I've always done it. I'd lose my place."

Abraham sat down again; this time it was Amelia who plucked at his sleeve and kept her hand on his arm long after Cadwallader had started to read again.

"First I want to say something to you, Mary Lee."

Her back went straighter, as if she had to sit stiff as iron to combat the woman when, for the first time, she couldn't talk back. Cadwallader went on, reading the last words in the argument, which Miss Anna Mary had simply insured by dying.

"*You've been a good girl in your own lights. You've taken over and run things, and made everything work for quite a while. In return I've given you a home. I'm not going to criticise the behaviour of a sick man like Longridge, but if he's as sick as all that, seems to me your best future is to go on home and look after him. Everybody'll get on all right here. There's lots of times I would have told you this, Mary Lee, but I had a selfish reason. I love that girl of yours. Mary Margaret reminds me of myself a way long time ago before I got myself a passel of youngins and then lost John and had to go killing snakes every day. I just couldn't sit by and see that youngin living with only you and a sick man and nobody to turn to when you bullied her.*"

Cadwallader felt, rather than heard the pressure of Mary Lee's anger, and his voice leapt ahead so that she'd find no gap to lash in and destroy his effort to finish the worst part of his job.

"*You always liked the sewing-machine. You can have that.*

The Kiss of Kin

You can have all the chickens except fifty White Leghorn spring pullets and a Leghorn rooster. They look prettier around the back yard and in my opinion they're the best fryers as well as layers. You can have that rocking-chair on the back porch to take home, too. It seems to belong to you in a way."

Cadwallader stopped reading, waiting for the crash of Mary Lee's anger. But nothing happened. She sat like a pillar of stone, staring in front of her, the only evidence that she had heard him at all was her hands, clutched in her lap until the knuckles were dead white.

They waited until her silence had cast a kind of fear in all of them worse than her violence would have done. Cadwallader spoke as if he were waking her up.

"Mary Lee. Mary Lee!" She dragged her eyes from staring to look at him.

"That's all about you, Mary Lee."

When she looked at him, it seemed to make her alive again and Cadwallader was almost relieved when she sprang half out of her chair and began to yell at him.

"How can you dare to stand there and tell me that the senile ravings of an ignorant old woman are legal? Don't you know your job? Haven't you got any sense?"

"Now, Mary Lee, you just please keep a little bit quieter and let me read the rest. I'm sure we can iron everything out at the end if we'll just keep calm."

Mary Lee sank back in her chair and closed her eyes. Cadwallader was so relieved he could hardly drag his mind back to the will, and took so long finding the place again that Cinnybug reached up and pushed at his arm. "Go on!" He found his place and began again.

"Now there's a little bit of money. Not so much as all of you thought there was gonna be so you might as well be prepared. The combined savings and assets come to eleven thousand three hundred and seventy-six dollars."

The Kiss of Kin

Cadwallader stopped and looked up to explain.

"There's an addition here, made last week. Only last week! Do you know, she never lost track of her property right up to the last. Never missed a trick."

"How much is it?" Amelia pulled him back to the point.

"The new figure is," he found the place and began to read again, "*sixteen thousand three hundred and fifty dollars. In addition I've kept an insurance policy to be divided between all my grandchildren, however many there are by the time I die.*"

Cadwallader stopped again to look up sadly. "You know, she's the only person I ever knew who put that word down, just like that, in a will. . . ." But when no one answered he went on, "*It's for three thousand dollars. Now there's three of you so far. Abraham, Mary Armstrong and John Junior.*"

Julik jerked his head round to Mary Margaret.

"*So that makes a thousand apiece. If any of you are under-age when I die, I want your share held for you until you are of age and then a cheque is to be handed to you which none of your parents has any say in the spending of it. People need a little pocket money with just their name on it.*"

Cadwallader paused here, and Abraham smiled and began to get up from his chair again, but Julik's loud whispering to Mary Margaret stopped him.

"You're left out. There's no money. Mary, what did I tell you? You might have listened . . ."

Cadwallader interrupted him. "Wait a minute, Mr. Rosen. Mary Margaret's next."

He found his place in the will again.

"*Now for Mary Margaret. You're going to have to stand for a little bit of fuss over what I'm going to say. After all, you aren't as close kin as the others. But I love you. I always did.*"

Mary Margaret felt for Julik's hand to hold it, but he'd

put both elbows on the table and was leaning forward, swallowing the words of the will as Cadwallader stumbled through them.

"*Now there's been a lot of things said about you lately, honey, but to show you I trust you and know that you wouldn't do anything to stain your girlhood,*"

Cinny bit her mouth together to keep a giggle, like a nervous tic, from forming at her mother's phrase. But she stopped when she heard the next sentence.

"*I'm leaving five thousand dollars to Mary Margaret Rosen, and I hope your marriage will always be happy.*"

Mary Margaret heard faintly a little cry from Cinnybug, and a sound from across the table, but she couldn't see. Her head was down, bowing in her lap, and she was crying a stream of tears, but silently, so that the rest, intent on Cadwallader after the first glances of surprise and anger at her, could not see. Only Julik, who had finished listening, sat back relaxed in his chair.

"*Now another five thousand dollars is to go to John.*"

Cadwallader looked up. "She told me to write and tell him and I've already done it." He looked down at the will again.

"*There's no use giving him a piece of the house when he's set on gallivanting around all over the place. He won't see a bit of use in a piece of farmhouse way out in the back woods. Write him my suggestion that he ought to send for his youngin. The boy needs him. Nothing good ever came of anybody that was raised entirely by women.*"

Cadwallader stopped. "I wrote him all that in the letter. Of course I told him how she said it was best for John Junior . . ."

But Cinny had counted up and she looked at Cadwallader, horrified, having no idea what he was talking about because . . .

The Kiss of Kin

"That's not enough! It's not enough! Cad, that only leaves six thousand dollars! Jellicoe, what . . ."

Cadwallader stopped her in mid-wailing, and she held her breath to listen . . .

"Now you wait a minute, Cinnybug." He found his place quickly this time and began to read again.

"*Now for the house.*"

The rest of the women swerved in their seats, and Cinny let her breath out loudly.

"*That's your house. The main thing, after all. I leave this house jointly to Amelia, Cinnybug (her real name is Thelma, I reckon I ought to put that in to make it legal), and to Abraham's son, the present Abraham Passmore.*"

The room was in its first uproar of the evening. Cadwallader had expected it. What he had not expected was Abraham's loud laughter over the lashing voices of the women. He went on loudly, and they quieted down again.

"*Here are the terms. It is to be owned jointly. None of you's to sell your share without consent of the others. In other words, it isn't sliced up, and one of you can't go off and sell up to some stranger. If you ever sell, you've got to agree.*"

Now the room was as still as it had been full of noise.

"*The rest of the money, six thousand three hundred and fifty dollars, is to be divided equally between the same three of you.*"

Cadwallader stumbled over the sum, and turned it slowly under the light, for Miss Anna Mary had done some of her figuring on the page, and crossed it out, so that Cadwallader, although he thought he'd memorised the figure, couldn't quite make it out, with the eyes on him, and the voices all ready to attack as soon as his own voice had stopped for a second to give them a chance.

So he kept on saying, "Wait a minute, just a minute now. Almost got it. Yes, that's the right figure." He saw a movement from Amelia out of the tail of his eye. "Wait a minute, Amelia, there's some more."

He found his place again. "*When I think of Abraham dying off out there somewhere, it pretty near breaks my heart. Well, his youngin's going to have a home to come to. He's got three thousand dollars, and now he's got a roof over his head. Little Abraham, it's what I would have done for your father, but he wouldn't let me—never wrote nor nothing. It's all I can think of to do for you, except to say I'm sorry we never did meet, and I hope you're like both your parents. I never did quite understand what all the fuss was about. If I had anything to do with it, I'm so sorry. But maybe I'll meet Abraham on the other side in God's Glory and tell him there wasn't no harm meant.*"

Abraham did lean forward then, till his shadow, under the top light, had split the table.

"Cad, stop. You've got to stop a minute!"

"There's not much more. It has to be read. All of it."

Abraham waited, standing, ready for the last words.

"*So youngins, it's the best I could do for you. I've tried to watch out for you and do what was right and also what wouldn't hurt you. May we meet in glory. Amelia, I wish you'd stop that terrible habit. Signed Anna Mary Passmore, witnessed Joab Wilson, Oliver Whitcome.*"

CHAPTER XV

ABRAHAM didn't move, and the silence, waiting for him to say what he had to, after all the impatience, got to the length that Jellicoe couldn't stand. He laughed and found something to say.

"Didn't know either one of them could write!"

In the silence after the witnesses' names had been read, A'nt Elemere roused herself from her own thoughts, which she was not prepared to voice, and from her comfortable fat wedge against the side of the sink, and began to pour the inevitable coffee and hand it round, passing it over arms that fell away from the table as she came near. Then she came to Cinny, who, coming alive, and throwing herself over in her chair, nearly upset the coffee cup.

"Jelly! Jelly! It isn't enough! It isn't enough! What are we going to do?"

"Now you know I'm not much good at this sort of thing, Cinnybug, I'd ask Cad if I was you."

Cinny turned to Cadwallader, accusing him.

"Cad, you told me I'd be all right. You told me last week!"

Cadwallader tried to pacify the quivering woman, who was turned, neck stretched, face half-grinning with fear, up into his face.

"Well, now, Cinny, that isn't a bad sum. The Passmore place is known to be one of the finest pieces of property in this county. Now you just think over how lucky you are."

Cinny's face was blotted with fear.

"I owe five thousand dollars to Mr. Crasscopper. I signed it! Signed it myself twenty-five years ago. It was all hinged on the fact I'd be remembered."

Cadwallader was fatherly with her, but a little shocked; for when it came to money, he knew where he stood and what was right and what wasn't and what was just plain sloppy.

"Now, Cinnybug, you told your mother that had been paid off down to two thousand dollars. That's what she left you this for."

Cinnybug found herself beginning to laugh, and hiccoughed for breath to shout, "Paid off! We haven't had our heads above water long enough ever!" But when she looked round at Jellicoe, sitting there all sorry and slack, she wailed, "Oh, Jelly, why can't you be some use?"

A'nt Elemere took her arm and put her down in her chair again, making her sit solid, making her drink something, whispering all the time, "Now come on, Miss Cinny, you just sit down there and drink your coffee."

Cinnybug did as she was told, but went on moaning still, "What are we going to do?"

Outside by the rain-barrel, the Reverend Beedie Jenkins slowly lifted his hat and pulled it down firmly over his eyes, so that even in the dark he tipped his head back slightly to pick his way along the path. It gave him a faint air of pride when his head was covered that he never had when his hat was clutched to his stomach and his head bent prayerwards.

He walked very slowly, and because he was completely alone he didn't even notice that the evidence of his feelings was falling down his sun-lined cheeks. He screwed up his eyes and his eyebrows hard to control his thoughts, but they came out anyway. He muttered to himself as he reached the gate, feeling for it in the darkness:

"Sister Anna Mary knowed me better'n that. She knowed me better'n that."

The Kiss of Kin

Brother Beedie forgot to be quiet, and slammed the gate behind him.

Abraham had not sat down again, but had stood, hovering over the table, waiting, still until there was a minute of peace for him to harrow. Now he spoke, but quietly: "Someone in this room tore up a letter from my mother to my grandmother. I want to know who it was."

They had all known trouble would come from him. But when the first of it did come, none of them caught the real sling of his question, they were so intent on their own troubles. The sound of his voice only reminded Cinnybug that he was there, and she looked up hopefully.

"Abraham, you've got money. If we could all agree maybe it would be all right." Then, with great effort, she smiled. "Maybe we could sell the house!"

Abraham no more heard her than she heard him; he was watching Mary Lee, who he knew had taken in what he'd said.

"Who tore up that letter?" He asked her, privately.

Mary Lee dismissed him. "I don't know what you're talking about."

He would have answered her but for the sudden noise as Julik jumped up and let his chair topple behind him. Abraham caught him poised, half-upright, trying to drag Mary Margaret to her feet. Then the whole picture moved. Julik was almost shouting for joy, "Come on, Mary, get the bags. We've got a train to catch!"

"What? What did you say?" She seemed drowsy with the shock of her news. "Is it time?"

"We've got to call the man who brought us from the station. There's no use sitting around here." Mary Margaret didn't answer. The silence Julik had created made him look from one to the other of them as they watched him. "Well, isn't it over? Isn't the whole thing over? What are we waiting for?" He tried to smile.

Mary Lee jumped up, shaking with anger, and ran round the table to bar his path.

"You wait, my friend, the whole thing has hardly begun!"

"Whoooom!" said Amelia, making a gesture like an explosion with her arms, ending with one hand patting Abraham's arm, absent-mindedly.

Mary Lee turned from Julik to Cadwallader.

"Cadwallader, can a will be broken if something isn't true. If it isn't true? You talked about the spirit . . . the spirit and the letter. . . ."

The question brought Mary Margaret to her feet, and she watched Mary Lee with such fascination at her that she was even without disgust.

"Mother!" Her voice was as soft as sighing.

"Well, can it?" Mary Lee motioned her to shut up.

Cadwallader was too upset to understand a word of what Mary Lee was saying. He'd figured it all out ahead of time, where the trouble would come from, who'd fight whom, and how he'd step between and what he'd have to do to keep the peace; but this was a thing he hadn't reckoned on, and to look at Mary Lee he could tell she was as near to having murder in her eye as ever he'd seen her.

"I don't quite get you, Mary Lee. Everything's very legal. Why Miss Anna Mary was as . . ."

"Look at what she said about Mary Margaret!"

Mary Margaret knew then that it was the end for whatever dreams she'd packed up and brought down and let loose in the house, and she sat down again, too defeated to more than half listen any more.

"Go on. Look at it. Go on."

"Well, here it is, Mary Lee. Look. Mary Margaret

The Kiss of Kin

Rosen. All legal. She'll get her money all right." He was relieved. There wasn't anything he'd done wrong. He put the will down on the table.

"That's not what I mean and you know it. What did the old fool say . . . 'stain her girlhood'? I'll throw that highfalutin talk back in both their damned faces." She swung round and asked the next question at Mary Margaret. "What if she wasn't married?" But Mary Margaret sat like a half-asleep girl, and didn't rise enough at the trouble to even look at her mother. Mary Lee leaned forward and began to pound at the will. "Wouldn't that put a different slant on the whole thing? Wouldn't it? Wouldn't that be what A'nt Anna Mary meant?"

"Well, now, let me see." Cad spoke slowly and picked the paper up again slowly, all to calm her down while he thought. He stared at the name, then took out a pencil, and put it back again into his pocket as he talked.

"I reckon the law would be that if it was left to Mary Margaret Rosen, and she wasn't Mary Margaret Rosen, but Mary Margaret Something Else—you know, a mistake. Well, I reckon . . ." He fiddled with the pencil in his pocket again.

"You reckon what?" Mary Lee's voice brought him back to the point, as cold and hard as a bit.

He took a deep breath and said what he had to.

"I reckon it would be that if that person named in the will was known by that name, well everybody would know who it meant. Wouldn't they?" Cadwallader asked hopefully. Now that he'd done what he had to, he turned and looked at Mary Lee, thinking he ought to make her understand. "But even if there was trouble you wouldn't get anything, Mary Lee. You see, you're not a direct heir." He could see as he told her that she knew already and that it wasn't the reason; the reason was something he'd never understand about. He waved both his arms, including them all, trying to get back to being a simple lawyer.

"But it's all right. I'm sure it's all right. I'm sure there's not going to be any trouble. We were so careful so there wouldn't be any trouble."

"What about the spirit? What about your fine spirit?" Mary Lee asked with a slight laugh.

Mary Margaret seemed to wake up, and she reached forward and tugged at Mary Lee's sleeve to make her turn round. But Julik had swallowed the trouble and gave her no time to speak. He turned on Cadwallader and began to yell.

"What's all this about? What's she talking about?"

Mary Margaret had attracted Mary Lee's attention.

"Mary Margaret, can you prove, can you swear and show proof that you are legally Mary Margaret Rosen? Are you married to this man?"

"No. I can't." Mary Lee, even standing above her, could hardly hear the answer, but she heard enough.

"I'm sorry. I can't."

Cadwallader leaned down to her, across the table.

"Mary Margaret, honey, I think you ought to have some legal advice. You don't want to lose your share, Miss Anna Mary'd of been awful upset. That phrase. It's kind of ambiguous. It crept in . . ." he ended, disappointed.

"Would she?" He couldn't hear her at all, only see her lips move.

Julik grabbed his arm and pulled him up straight to have it out.

"But a phrase! Some corny old woman's words! It can't stand between Mary and what's due to her!"

But Cadwallader didn't have time to answer. Mary

Lee had finally lost control and she pushed her face into his, spitting at him.

"I don't know about your kind of people, but in this family a word can stand for quite a lot. That word is marriage." She jerked round to Mary Margaret, bending closer and closer until she was close enough for the girl to see the spittle clogged between her false teeth and her gums.

"Do you mean to tell me you thought you could get by with flaunting yourself, nothing but showing yourself, nothing but acting as if you was naked in front of people! Dirty! Naked!"

"Stop her," Mary Margaret finally began to cry. "Somebody stop her!"

"Shut up, Mary!" Julik yelled at her over Mary Lee's anger and made them both turn towards him. But he spoke only to Cadwallader, who had the disaster in the palm of his hand.

"Let's get this straight. Wilson, is it true?"

If there was one thing in the world that made Cadwallader's blood rise above snake level, it was to be called by the wrong name. Julik had lost his last champion.

"My name, sir, is Williams," Cadwallader told him.

Julik only waited for his mouth to stop moving.

"Can Mary Margaret be kept from what's rightfully hers by a trick like this?"

"Well, now, Mr. Rosen, I know you've got Mary Margaret's interests at heart, but I don't think you ought to take on like that about it. There's no trick. There's certainly no trick. Just one of those unfortunate mistakes." He kept reading and rubbing at the will as if the words had changed into another language before his eyes.

"You mean she won't get anything at all?" Julik was so horrified that his voice squeaked like a little boy's.

The Kiss of Kin

Cadwallader cleared his throat carefully to gain time and calm everything down. "Well, I wouldn't put it like that, Mr. Rosen. No." He thought for a second, holding his breath. "No. Not just like that. It might mean that at the worst of course. It certainly means litigation." He sat down for the first time since the will-reading, as if the word had won and pushed him there.

"Litigation," he repeated sadly. "Long, drawn-out, expensive litigation. Maybe months. Oh Lord! I'm not clear on that point. I'm just not clear on that point." He hitched up his glasses with his knuckles and rubbed his dry eyes. Then he remembered he was talking to the strange young man. "I'm mighty sorry about this, wouldn't have had it happen for the world. But you see, if you could produce your marriage licence, everything would be straightened out in no time." This prospect cheered Cadwallader a little and made him sit up in his chair.

Mary Lee, frozen like a statue, stood looking somewhere over Julik's shoulder. Now she brought her eyes back to him and smiled, but said nothing.

Suddenly he was nearly crying, his throat tight with it. "I knew it would happen. I knew something like this would happen. I felt it coming! You're all glad, aren't you? You think I'm not good enough to touch your money!" He knew he was doing just what they would have expected him to do, but he went right on, hating them, loathing them, looking from face to lazy face, and hardly seeing them. "Aren't you satisfied now that a trick's been played?"

Cadwallader got to his feet again, insulted.

"Mr. Rosen, there was no trick. I wouldn't do a thing like that. It isn't ethical. I carried out the wishes of..."

"Ethical?" Julik looked at Cadwallader as if he wondered if he were quite sane. "Look, mister. Tell me something." He began to yell again and nearly choked. "What do you people know about ethical? What do you know about it? Where does ethical come to a man wanting something all his life and not able to get it? Where's the ethical, I'm asking you?"

He couldn't look any more at Cadwallader's long, grey face; he tried to focus on the others, at Jellicoe's flabby face, at Amelia, with a half-grin she'd left and forgotten, at Cinnybug, twisting and turning and obviously waiting for him to shut up and get out.

"Which one of you ever had any ambition to get someplace? Oh Jesus!" His oath was a cry. "Something like this would happen to me!"

Mary Margaret interrupted before he could say any more. "Julie. Oh, please, Julie . . ." She seemed to be moaning instead of speaking.

The sound of it stopped him at last. His terrible disappointment blotted out his anger and he was left high and dry, feeling hardly alive. He started for the door.

"O.K. O.K. I'll get our bags." He pushed it open and walked out without looking at her. It was only when he disappeared into the dining-room that Mary Margaret could make herself move at all. She jumped up and ran after him, catching the door with her shoulder as it swung back.

"Julie," she called by habit. "You can't lift those things."

Then she stopped on her way after him through the dining-room, and leaned against the wall as if she were too tired to move another step.

"What does it matter now?" He turned back to wait for her. "What does it matter about my hands? Don't just stand there." When she didn't move for him he called sharply, "Mary!"

"You go on, honey." She turned her face to the wall.

He wanted to shake her, but took her arm instead and tried to drag her along. "Mary, don't cause any more trouble. You don't expect me to spend the night in this hole, do you?"

She shook away from him. "No. You go on."

"Look, Mary, what's the matter?"

"Nothing. I'm not coming, that's all." All the trouble had set her back, like a little girl, and from the look on her face he knew there'd be trouble trying to reason with her.

"Mary, come on now. Just move on. Come on upstairs." He piloted her by the arm, and it wasn't until she set foot on the lowest step that she stopped again. "I just don't want to." She bit her lip, worried.

"Now, Mary, don't talk like that. You come on upstairs. We'll be on the train in a little while. Won't that be nice?" He found himself playing a crazy child game with her, just to get her to move on.

"I don't want to," she kept on saying as he took her up the stairs. "Everybody needs me and nobody wants me. I want to sit down."

It was like piloting a drunk. "Now don't you talk like that, Mary. What would I do without you?" He sat her down in the rocking-chair of their bedroom, then she remembered to say:

"Julie, I'm very sorry."

Looking at her, he realised at last that she was serious.

"Look, Mary, you can't do this to me right now. You just can't do it. After all I've suffered today I can't stand it. Haven't you got any feelings?"

"I'm sorry, Julie," she said again, and covered her eyes, even though it was night and both of them had forgotten to turn on the light, but had let the shaft from the hall guide them. "Oh, it doesn't matter," she mumbled into her hand.

"Christ, Mary, I can't stand this." Julik lurched down towards her. "I can't stand any more. Christ, don't you realise I'm thirty-four years old!" He fell against her legs and hung there in the air, trying to get his balance back. She wanted to pull her skirt away to free herself, but dared not, knowing how near he was to tears.

CHAPTER XVI

AS the dining-room door swung shut, Mary Lee began to move. She sat down in Mary Margaret's chair.

"I knew it. I knew they weren't married!"

Abraham leaned towards her, almost sick with disgust at her.

"You know a lot, don't you? Poor bugger! He asked for trouble and you were the girl who knew how to give it to him!"

Mary Lee started to speak, but Cinnybug had waited long enough for her answer from Abraham, with people interrupting and taking his mind off the important thing all the time.

"Abraham! If we could sell?"

But it was Amelia who interrupted and answered her before Abraham had a chance, leaning across the table until she was almost lying down.

"What about me? What if I won't sell?"

Cinny looked at her, surprised, wondering if the expression round Amelia's mouth was a smile, part of a joke or something.

"But, Amelia! You always did want a little money to start up something for yourself!"

Amelia laid her head down the little bit more until it was lying sideways on her arm.

"Thelma, look at me." She stopped smiling, or whatever it was.

"Look at me!" She raised her head, swaying a little, and sat watching Cinny. "Don't I just look like somebody who could pick up lock, stock and barrel and start on my own. Now, don't I?" Her mouth turned down at the edges. "Look at me!" She lunged forward with her final question. "Why do you think Mother left me a home?"

"But ever since Charles Truxton Edwards died, you been . . ."

Amelia took a deep breath.

"Charles Truxton Edwards was a son of a bitch!" she said, and then she laid her head down between her arms on the table.

Cinny swung back to Abraham.

"Abraham, persuade her! Please persuade her!"

His face was as cold as Amelia's had been bitter.

"Why should I?"

She clutched at the edge of the table and pulled herself up towards him.

"But you don't need this place! You've got money!"

He was so quiet for a big man that, when he answered her the way he did, Cinny thought for a minute that he'd come round to her way of thinking, and she sat back.

"You seem to have forgotten something. All of you have. I came down here for a certain reason. If there's a score to pay, I'll pay it. I want the truth. Then I'll decide what can become of my part of this."

But if his stillness had fooled Cinnybug, it had been like a red flag of danger for Cadwallader, still trying desperately to make everything go smooth, by refusing to recognise its going any other way.

"Abraham, I don't think this is quite the time . . ."

Abraham's angry interruption showed even Cinnybug she'd made a mistake.

"This is exactly the time. Williams, read that first part of my grandmother's will again. I want you all to listen."

Cadwallader unfolded the will and began to look over it, humbling in his throat for a call to order as he looked.

"Now, let me see. Let me see. Where is it you want?"

The Kiss of Kin

Abraham's finger jabbed to so exact a place that Cad's eyes had to be pinned to it. "There. Read it. Read it out."

Cadwallader wiggled the corner of his glasses by habit, humbled again in his throat, stalling just a few seconds more. Then he began to read again.

"*If I could of imagined in all my born days that I never was going to lay eyes on Abraham or hear from him again, I don't think I could of stood it. But there comes times when you have to face up to things. This morning I've got to face up to the fact that I won't see Abraham until I get to the other side. Ignorance makes you foolish. . .*" Cad looked up to see if he'd read enough, but Abraham said:

"Go on."

He found his place. "*. . . makes you foolish; makes you stand for too much sometimes. I waited too long for that boy of mine to write to me. He went away mad. He had a reason . . .*"

"That's enough."

Mary Lee sucked her teeth. "We've heard all that before." She got up to go out on to the porch. Abraham was ahead of her, holding her close. From where Jellicoe sat, bored half to death, they looked like they were dancing. He wanted to turn it into some joke, but dared not with Cinnybug all hot and bothered as she was. He heard Abraham say to Mary Lee, "No you don't, sister." He pushed her back towards the table. Jellicoe lost interest.

"Six months before my father died, he wrote a letter to my grandmother. After he got sick, my mother wrote again. I helped her to write it. As you all know, she couldn't write English very well." He walked towards Mary Lee, his voice edged, as bitter as Julik's had been.

"Somebody here destroyed those letters before my

grandmother saw them." Then he was looking at Mary Lee and at no one else. "I want to know who it was."

"What do you think we are?" Mary Lee saw her chance, catching the quality like Julik in him, an Achilles heel.

But it wasn't going to work.

"Who did it?"

"Don't you use that tone of voice with me!"

"Who did it, goddamn you?"

She said nothing. Neither did anyone else.

Abraham let his own voice drop low. "Until I find out, I'm going to let the Passmore place sink and all of you with it."

Cinnybug found her voice and used it to accuse.

"This is all your fault! This is your fault, Mary Lee!"

Mary Lee stood her ground.

"I don't know what she's raving about." She turned to glare at Cinnybug, and her look made Cinny close her mouth with a snap. Then Mary Lee turned back to Abraham and took a stand to lay down the law on him.

"Listen here, young man, if you thought we were going to stand by and see Abe crawl to his mother behind our backs, you're vastly mistaken." She stopped, waiting to hear what he'd say, but when he didn't speak she baited him again.

"If he got his comuppins from being so high and mighty with us, then it wasn't any of our business."

Then Abraham found a way to say what had been on his mind from the first, what he was there to let them all know.

"If she'd ever seen those letters, he wouldn't have died."

Mary Lee's rage flamed up at him for it.

"That's just your mother in you coming out." She looked round the table for someone to agree with what she said, someone to back her up in her injured innocence. "Blaming us for something when we didn't even know anything about it. Did you ever hear tell? Isn't it just like her?"

But when no one answered she turned back. "We didn't know a damn thing about it." Then, to stop the silence that followed, "You act like we up and killed him!"

"You did!" Abraham bawled it at her, and then stood shaking, looking from one to the other of them.

"My father died because he couldn't pay for decent care."

No one answered a word. He walked to the screen-door, back again, pulled back his chair beside Amelia and sat down, all slowly, getting himself back into contact with them, and when he finally told them the rest, it was as if he were telling a story that hadn't happened, it seemed so far from him.

"A sick man can't hold a job for long. My mother went to work to look after him. He didn't ever want her to, but she couldn't do anything else, with him so sick. Well, it only made him get worse and worse. There seemed to be something in him, something heavy he never threw off, that kept him ever from getting on top of his sickness. I've always thought whatever it was came from here. Or maybe it was the war. Anyway, it was on account of her he finally asked for some help from his mother. When he got no answer he wouldn't try any more. Then she tried."

Mary Lee took in a gasp of breath to speak, but when Abraham looked up at her, she changed her mind.

"When he died, the doctor told my mother that. He told her that, standing in the room there with him. I was standing in the door and I heard him say it. 'Tuberculosis is a strange disease,' is what he told her. 'If he had had enough to eat and the right kind of care, he mightn't have died.' 'He gave in,' she was saying. 'He gave . . .'"

Mary Lee could stand it no longer. She destroyed the silence while Abraham recalled the story, with a critical, sentiment-damning snort. "Oh, mighty pitiful! Mighty long-winded and pitiful! So she thought if she sent you down here with a tale like that she could get something out of us anyway. Do you think we were born yesterday?"

Abraham was patient with her. "Now you don't need to worry about her. She died soon after he did. You can't share a bed with a man with T.B. . . ." But he stood up to face her, stretching himself, as if the moment had finally come to hear and not to tell.

"I was fifteen years old when Dad died. Some way I escaped it. And I've been waiting ever since to find out something. I want to know the trouble, all the way back. I want to know what happened to the letters. . . ."

"Go on, Mary Lee, tell him!" Amelia called at her. She grinned. "Or do you want me to?"

"All right. I'll tell you. I burned the letters. Now. Are you satisfied? Got what you come here for? I burned them."

But he left her to explain as she'd left him to, isolated, surrounded by watchers.

"I knew who they were from the minute I laid eyes on them. I knew they'd just be some begging stuff, and I didn't see a bit of sense dragging everything up again and worrying your grandmother. God knows she was worried enough with all the trifling family she had; I reckoned that if she got rid of one of them she ought to stay rid of him. Him and that woman!" Mary Lee's mouth curled into the smile of a woman who had heard the joke before. "Imagine! Trying to just come back and sit on their haunches . . ."

Abraham grabbed her arm to pull her to him across the table, but when he felt its frailty he dropped it again.

"I don't get it," he said so quietly that she thought all the anger had gone out of him, and kept on smiling. "All over America there are women like you. We raise our women in a hard soil and sometimes one of them goes crazy—" he watched her closely as if he could read the answer in the lines of her face. "She goes crazy with sadistic self-confidence and moral superiority. Nobody locks her up! They just hand her the reins and let her run things. . . ."

"If you know so much . . ." she began, but he wouldn't let her tell him.

"What in the name of God made you think you had a right to do a thing like that?"

"It was the right thing for me to do," she told him. "If you had any idea of the responsibility I had to shoulder . . ." but she didn't finish when she saw the way he looked at her.

He was too amazed, when he realised that nothing he'd ever say would make her see what she'd done, even to raise his voice. "So help me, you're too far gone for me even to want to punish you!"

"I don't care what you do." She walked past him close to him, but stopped when she got to the screen-door and was holding it open. "Why should I give a damn what youall do? This family can't do any more to me than they've done already." She was nearly crying, but they were tears of anger, not of grief. "I've worked my fingers to the bone and all the thanks I get is to be forgotten." She went out, trying to slam the door behind her, but it wouldn't slam. The screen only made a light complaining sound. They could hear the creak of the rocker as she sat down, but it was pitch-dark by then and she was lost to sight.

Cadwallader took advantage of her going to try to pull the meeting together, hoping to God that Abraham had stirred up enough trouble to satisfy whatever it was he wanted fed.

"Now I'm sure we can all come to some understanding, Cousin Abraham." He picked up the will again to remind them, and because it was all more businesslike if somebody had a paper in his hand. He slapped it against the table to get attention.

"Now, please, everybody, let's get down to brass tacks. After all, there's always a peaceful way to settle a thing if we just set ourselves to try and find it."

But when Abraham cut back to him, he knew that he had failed already.

"I want the rest of the story." He went close to Cadwallader, explaining.

"Now, look here, boy," Cad tried for the last time to stop him. "Now I'm sure a little falling out a long time ago couldn't mean so much to you. You were only a little boy, hardly dry behind the ears. Now you come on . . ."

Abraham shook him off and pushed him aside as if he were a curtain, gently. "Look, I want the whole story." He walked round the table. "You tell me, A'nt Amelia. I'd like to hear it from you." He leaned down to her, perched on a chair with one foot, leaning, getting nearer and nearer her face. "I'm sure that, in your present state, telling me a lot of fancy lies would seem a little silly."

But she didn't look at him. "Don't remember."

"Yes, you do." He let himself down, astride the chair, watching her closely, trying to draw the story out. "Now I've always remembered one thing. This kitchen, but not like this . . ." he looked around, still surprised a little at the difference. "Everything in it used to be tall. There was a flutter of white dresses."

He caught something winging past in her memory.

"White dresses. That must have been the summer I came home to stay . . ."

"Where was Charles Truxton?"

She was bitter. "He lost his job. One of his jobs. He was looking around. I stayed here." She turned round, forgetting what it was all about, just trying to remember and gossip with him.

"You were still here, knee-high to a duck. You and your mother. We all wore white dresses, with little tucks in the front. Thousands of little hand-made tucks." She fingered the front of her black dress, as if she'd conjure up the rippling touch of them.

"Thousands of them. All hand-stitched. Seem to spend half our time washing and ironing white dresses. Clothes were a lot prettier then."

She caught his eye, and knew with a gust of sober sense what he was up to. She shut up and let her voice slur back to the evening's normal.

"That's all I remember."

"I don't believe you." He said it so gently she was almost fooled.

"I said that's all I remember, Mister Smart!"

CHAPTER XVII

EVEN Abraham stopped at the sound of the back screen-door.

Mary Margaret had opened it slowly, and she let it slide as slowly closed through her hand when she stepped through. She was alone.

She came and sat down again at the table, and Abraham asked her what they all were waiting to hear:

"Where's Julik Rosen?"

"He's gone."

Cinnybug laughed. "Gone? Where would he go? Number Nine doesn't come through till ten-fifteen."

Mary Margaret brushed her voice aside. "He's going to wait at the station."

Amelia began to roar with laughter, partly from relief because Mary Margaret had stopped Abraham getting nearer than he knew to her.

"I'd like to see that trifling bunch down at the depot when Mr. Rosen runs up with a chip on his shoulder and his hands in a flower muff." She bent forward, double, on the table, groaning with laughter.

Mary Margaret raised her voice for the first time then since the night had begun. She jumped up.

"Stop it, A'nt Amelia. Everybody can't be like you!"

Amelia stopped laughing, suddenly. A'nt Elemere, who had started to pour coffee when she saw Mary Margaret come back, brought it to her and pushed her back towards her chair.

"Here, drink your coffee and let your a'nt alone."

"I hate that attitude." Mary Margaret stood still looking at Amelia.

"Come on now, honey." She sat down, slackly.

Abraham came round the table and stood over her, forgetting, or not caring, that the others were there at all.

"So you've left him." He said it like the tag line of an old joke.

"I'm staying here for a few days," she murmured, not looking up at him.

But he took her by the shoulders and turned her to him, laughing at her in a way Amelia hadn't done.

"Move over all the Marys! Here comes another Mary!" He shoved her back into her chair.

"Take your place at the kitchen table. Drink away your life in coffee. Failures Row, Ladies only!"

He left her alone and went back to where he'd come from across the table. She thought he'd forgotten her till he leaned over and told her quietly.

"A few days! You've come home to roost!"

She looked up at him of her own accord then, defending herself.

"Where else can I go right now?"

"Go?" He was too excited to come away around the table again to tell her, so he went on leaning across, then sat on the table edge, telling her.

"Go to a hotel. Get yourself a room. Get a bottle of licker too and get like A'nt Amelia here if that does any good. You're starting out on a new life! You can't do it back here curled up in your Kiddie Koop." Then to the point. "Have you got any money, sweetie?" He was close enough to pull her head to his and kiss her, but he straightened up again.

"Oh, what's the use?"

She had forgotten his laughter for a minute and her face was alive again.

"Does it take long?"

"What? Oh—a second. That much time. You don't know. You're lost, strayed, not worth stealing. Then bingo! Like that! You know."

It was all beyond Cinny and she didn't care, and her whole tense body unwound like a catapult. She sprang up and yelled at Cadwallader.

"This is a business meeting!"

Abraham looked round at her, and then sat down again on the edge of the table, his body between her and Cadwallader so that she couldn't see anything else but him.

"All right, A'ntie, I told you I meant business. My business is a past to learn about. I don't know any more than I did when I came except that my grandmother was not responsible for my father's death." He turned to Cadwallader and pointed his finger. "Put it down. Item One on the agenda. Put it down in the minutes." He sat owning the table, watching all of them.

"Now. I want to know the answer to the next question on the agenda." He lashed at Cinny, who was sitting quaking with frustration and trying to get a word in.

"Who kicked my mother out of this house, and why did they do it?"

So when the words came they were an answer, not the question she'd planned, and a half tearful answer at that.

"We didn't kick her out. She left of her own free will." Cinny looked round wildly for someone to back her up. But there was only Amelia. "Didn't she, Amelia? Didn't she?"

Abraham leaned down to Amelia then, too, and shook her, hard, trying to make her talk.

"Was there a row? What kind of a row? Why? Go on, why?"

Mary Lee could be heard getting up from her rocker in

the dark. She strode in straight as a knife, looking like a woman with her mind made up. Abraham saw her over Amelia's bent shoulder, and let go of it, letting her fall back into her slouch again.

"Miss Burden on the Shoulders!" He went to meet her, but she walked past him to the table.

"You couldn't stay out there on your high horse for long, could you? You might miss something."

She stopped and stood rigid against the table.

"Sit down." Abraham followed close to her. "This is a business meeting. A'nt Cinny likes it better that way."

She didn't look at him, but said instead, watching the others, turning her head slowly, forcing agreement:

"I've made up my mind. I've decided to tell him."

No one answered her, but Cinny began to get up without knowing it, and sat down again. Amelia's head rose slowly from her arms.

"I'm going to tell him."

Mary Lee turned to where Abraham stood, waiting for what he'd come for.

"You are a bastard."

"Mary Lee, that isn't true!" Cinny wailed at the lie with some relief because Mary Lee hadn't said what she'd thought she was going to.

"So far as we know, it is." Mary Lee didn't bother to look at her, but kept on, quietly, at Abraham, making him stand there in front of her in the middle of the kitchen floor and take all she'd been meaning to say for a long time.

"Well, if you're so hell-bent on knowing, here it is. We got a white girl in. God knows it was a mistake, but the niggers got so trifling during the first war, just like they did this one, and we had to do something. The one we got spoke about ten words of English."

Amelia smiled. "She was pretty, in a kind of way."

"I don't know about that." Mary Lee went on, never taking her eyes off Abraham, saying the truth so hard that she didn't even bother with anger, plastering him with the truth, if that's what he wanted.

"She wasn't our kind of people. Well, she didn't need more than ten words of English to do what she set herself to do to your father. According to them they sneaked away and got married before he went overseas." She sucked her teeth for a second, remembering.

"A'nt Anna Mary always acted like she believed it, but I don't for a minute think she did. I'm sorry to have to tell you this kind of thing but you asked for it." Now in spite of herself her voice began to rise.

". . . I'm sick and tired of hearing you complain around the house." She jerked her head towards the back screen-door. "You've not stopped since you set foot inside that door!"

"Go on." Abraham dragged her back to the story.

"Well, she moped and sulked around after he left." Mary Lee wasn't telling it so well now, for the venom in her memory was making her re-live what she was telling, slurring her voice, creasing her face.

"She wasn't one bit of good. She'd been taken out of her place and I reckon she found it a little unfair to get put back into it."

Abraham was held still by amazement at the woman.

"But you could do that?"

Mary Lee sucked her teeth, slowly, and half turned, dismissing him. "I certainly could." She started to pull a chair back to sit down.

"My God!" He watched her like you watch a snake.

She plopped herself down in the chair and sighed, bored with him.

The Kiss of Kin

"Now you don't need to start that ghostly surprise act. It's just your father come out in you. He always did try to get what he wanted that way." She sniggered a little. "Didn't he, Amelia?"

Abraham stopped them all by shouting:

"I'm not a person with a purpose here! I'm a document! This little piece is a bit of my father; this of my mother; this of my Uncle Joshuay; this of my A'nt Susanna." He paced around, forgetting them, but still shouting.

"As far as you people are concerned I'm only a proof that my father, my mother, my aunts, my uncles, my little grey cousins, all lived and worked and had their being!"

Mary Lee knew of a final thing to say to shut the loud-mouthed man up and get back to business and she stood up and stopped his ranting.

"Do you want to hear the rest of the story?"

She had shut him up, and as he waited for what she was going to say, she let him stand there again, just waiting, until she knew she had him where she wanted him.

"Or are you changing the subject because you are finding it isn't the pitiful little yarn you were led to believe?"

She was enjoying herself, throwing remarks at him, making him wait.

"It's just what I expected." Something in his voice made her go on, pell-mell, at the rest of it.

"Well, in a few months it wasn't hard for any durn fool to see what was making the girl mope. You were born eight months after your father left. If you didn't look like the spit of him . . ." She turned away again, finished with him, just making comments almost to herself as she sat down. ". . . I wouldn't be sure you were even his son . . ."

The Kiss of Kin

Abraham caught her such a swinging slap with his flat hand against her ear that he knocked her sideways into Mary Margaret's lap. The slap brought them all to their feet, watching. But no one came to help her. No one said a word, waiting in the silence after the slap as loud as the slamming of a door. Abraham leaned over her, almost whispering, his voice shaking with rage:

"Then what did you do?" But when she didn't answer, just lay in Mary Margaret's lap, stroking the side of her head where the hairpins had jammed and he had slapped a grey braid loose, he dragged her up to her feet again, like a full sack, holding her close to his face.

"What did you do to her? I want it all."

"Nothing! Nothing!" Mary Lee was slobbering and she tried to turn her head away, to take in the others. "Somebody make him stop!" But he jerked her head back to him. "Nothing!" Mary Lee screamed again. "We didn't even speak to the girl. We never said a word."

Abraham dropped her and she nearly fell, clutched a chair and dragged herself on to it, crying and trying to do up her hair, poking pins into her crying mouth without realising what she was doing.

"Not a word." Abraham walked close to the table, so gentle they all thought he hadn't heard her, until they listened to what he had to say.

"That's the part I know. She used to say to me, 'Don't stand there, like one of them. Say something. Anything. Even if you hate a man enough to kill him, talk. Silence full of words is the worst form of hatred.' She would say it was the only thing she knew that could drive a person crazy. But she would never tell me how she knew such a thing."

No one dared to answer him; they knew from watching him he wasn't finished, even though he was silent for such a long time that Mary Lee looked up, out of her misery, her mouth full of pins, wondering what was coming.

His head went slowly back as if it were being pulled, and he opened his mouth wide and yelled like a shouting Baptist:

"So help me God, I'll let this house and all that's in it rot to pieces if it takes my last cent tying it up in court!"

Cinny screamed first, fighting her way to Cadwallader.

"Can he do that? Cad! Can he?"

And Cadwallader's voice, even over hers, trying to keep the peace . . .

"Well, now, wait a minute, Abraham. That was a long time ago!"

Abraham's head came down, and he bent over Mary Lee, the tears streaming down his face but without a sob in his voice.

"Why did you do it? Why did you do it to that poor lonesome woman?"

The pins dropped out of her mouth and she spoke fast, words tumbling out too, explaining.

"She was poor white trash. We didn't have much money. Something had to be done. We couldn't have a scandal among the girls, and A'nt Anna Mary wouldn't hear of not having her right in with us after she knew about the baby. She just couldn't understand how important it was."

"What was? Come on, what was?" He held her by the arms again, shaking the real reason out of her. It came out yelling him down.

"Cinnybug was courting! She was courting! We couldn't have hired help sitting at the dinner table!"

"So you made it so she wouldn't want to."

"That was her own choice!" Her yell finally unleashed the others. Abraham stood back away from her and watched them scream at each other like gulls, Cinny's voice rising high over the rest, a soprano chant.

"You did it. You did it. You started it."

Then her voice swept under the general noise. Cadwallader stood over them, waving his hands for some kind of dignity in the whole thing, but they couldn't hear him nor see his lips move loosely, begging. Jellicoe, unaccountably, flicked a match under the table and made a patch of bright light, lighting a cigarette, ignoring the women face to face, tearing at each other in the middle of the table.

"Mary Lee, you started it!" Cinny's voice won again. "You said not to talk to her. You said she'd soon learn her place. We didn't mean to do any harm." She turned to appeal to Abraham, and he caught at her and tugged her away from the rest, looking past her down at Jellicoe.

"Do you mean to tell me you nearly ruined my mother's life so you could catch this man?"

There was still so much noise that Jellicoe didn't know he was being talked about. He blew out smoke and wiggled with boredom in his chair. Cinny watched him, then burst into tears.

"Stop it. Stop it, Abraham!" She sat down, feeling for a handkerchief. "When we were courting, Jellicoe was the cutest boy in this valley. He was the cutest and he had a car, and he promised to take me on a honeymoon none of the other boys would of. It wasn't our fault things didn't go according to plan! It's all right for you . . ." She waved her handkerchief at Abraham, then began to twist it, stopping her crying and looking at Jellicoe as if he were a stranger. "Everybody thought I was real lucky." She looked, completely puzzled, at her knotted handkerchief.

The Kiss of Kin

Abraham stood away from them until Mary Lee's and Amelia's voices ran down, and they leaned back exhausted into their chairs, as if they had been lovers instead of hell-catting at each other over the table-top, repeating and repeating accusations at each other, tiring themselves out.

Abraham caught Mary Margaret's eye. She sat there as still as she could be, with Mary Lee leaning half against her again. He looked away from her, to Jellicoe, to Cinny, still twisting and sniffling, to Amelia, on to Cadwallader.

"The family! Miss Anna Mary's family! Hold them together! Make them multiply! Keep them all eating out of the same trough no matter what it costs! If she had known what you were she'd never have tried to put a legal lock on our hating each other's guts. It'll take more than a letter from a tough old bitch to make us love each other. It'll take a goddamn miracle." He ended, looking at Amelia.

"Were you in it, too?"

Cinny flapped at her with the knot of handkerchief.

"Yes, she was. She was in it the same as the rest."

He turned to Mary Lee.

"And you. You were the ringleader. All in a woman's way, in the time women like best. Sewing! Rocking! Peeling potatoes! I can see it all so well."

He called Cadwallader back to power as gently as if he were asleep, instead of waiting to take over as impatient as a nervous man mounting a merry-go-round.

"Cad."

Only Amelia saw something in the way he said it of what he was thinking. She jumped up, yelling, frightened.

"What are you going to do?"

But he was still as gentle as ever, even when he said:

The Kiss of Kin

"I'm going to pay my mother back for all this family has done to her."

Then Cinny screamed, "What are you going to do?"

But he still didn't raise his voice.

"I own a third of this house and everything in it. From tomorrow morning I forbid the use of my third. My third of the chicken will die. My third of the cows will starve and take your two-thirds with it." He came close to Mary Lee.

"Try sitting and gloating on two-thirds of a rocking-chair," he called across the table.

"Lie awake nights thinking about it on two-thirds of a bed, hugging and beating two-thirds of a pillow!"

Mary Lee sprang at him and would have scratched his face, but he caught her hands.

"You fiend. You dirty fiend," she kept saying, trying to twist away.

"Don't blame me, sister." He pushed her down into her chair by her wrists. "It's the Mary Amelia Thelma Annie Coxey's Army Passmore coming out in me."

Cinnybug forgot even to cry. She tugged at Cadwallader's coat, jerking at every word, "Can he do it, Cousin Cad? Can he do it?"

He pulled himself loose.

"Of course he can't do it. He won't succeed." But nobody was listening to him, and he said to himself, sadly, "Oh, Lordy, why couldn't this all of been a little bit quieter?"

"I can't do it!" Abraham threw the law back in Cadwallader's face. "Of course I can't do it after it gets to the courts, but I can tie it up in court until the damage is done. I can do that and you know it."

He turned away from the table, through with them at last; when A'nt Elemere touched his arm as he passed, he shook even her away, and leaned his head against the screen, waiting, but too tired to think at all, just letting the sounds of the frogs croaking away down by the creek get to him and make a steady watery sound around him, resting in it, letting it engulf the women's voices behind him until they almost faded away.

Behind him at the table they'd run down, stuck, looking from one to the other, far too deep in trouble now to start accusing wildly at each other. Gradually, looking around, all three women's eyes lit on Cadwallader and stayed there. Cinnybug gulped quickly and got her words in first.

"Cadwallader, what did you let mother do it for? She musta been insane!"

Amelia's eyes were bright with tears, but she couldn't let them go, and her voice when she spoke was hard.

"She always was hard on us. You know that, Cad."

But before Cadwallader could defend himself or Miss Anna Mary, Cinny had broken in again, her voice beginning its steady rise.

"What are we gonna do?"

Amelia charged up, swinging the tears down out of her eyes, her voice breaking.

"Damn her! Damn Mother! Just like her, just like Charles Truxton, dying off without leaving me fixed."

Mary Lee was carefully buttoning her blouse at the wrists, but she looked up to interrupt. "You always knew your mother was turning into an old fool. Why'd you let her get away with it?"

She slapped her buttoned wrist.

"If youall had of listened to me, this never would of happened. I would of made quite certain she never get by with anything!"

It was her voice, rising over the others that made Abraham turn round, but the first thing he noticed was Mary Margaret, jumping up so quickly that she knocked her chair to the floor. This time her voice had lost its tight-rope balance and she was yelling louder than her mother.

"Leave her alone. Leave my grandmother alone."

She'd stopped their mouths, but not for long. Cinnybug set her right.

"She's not your grandmother. We've had just about enough of this grandmother . . ."

"Shut up, A'nt Cinny." Cinny's mouth gaped open. "Yes, I said shut up to you. I wondered when youall would start on her. You just leave her alone," she repeated, having stopped them, as if the words were magic to keep them quiet. Mary Lee had had enough of her little tantrum.

"You're in it the same as them. I don't know what you're blowing off your big bazoo for . . ."

"No, I'm not. I'm not staying here." She quit the table, leaving them, and ran towards Abraham, talking all the time.

"I'm going off tonight with Abraham. If he doesn't want me, he can drop me off beside the depot. Will you take me? Abraham, can I go with you?"

She couldn't notice that Mary Lee's face was going tight and dark, that she was being driven up from the table by her anger, for Cinnybug had squeaked at her, amazed, and she turned to look at her.

"Where would you go to?" Cinny was fascinated, watching her, big-eyed.

Mary Margaret burst into laughter at the look on her face, and couldn't answer her for laughing. Rather like a leaf that the wind of all the kitchen fury had disturbed, she swung crazily from one to the other of them, trying to stop her helpless laughter.

Amelia just shook her head back and forth.

"She's drunk."

"It's so funny!" Mary Margaret explained to Abraham through the laughter. He pulled her against him to quiet her, nearly upsetting them both.

"Take it easy," he almost whispered to her, and she was still.

Mary Lee's hard fingers bit into her arm and whirled her around from him. She was stiff, spitting, and her voice was tight and low.

"You'd do that? You'd do that? Flaunt yourself like that? I never expected any better of you."

Mary Margaret took away the hand from her arm, tore it away as if she were pulling a leech.

"Maybe that's why you never got any better."

Mary Lee stood stranded, not answering, the fear broken. Over Mary Margaret's shoulder, Abraham noticed for the first time that she had to look up to look into Mary Margaret's eyes. She looked sick and lonely and stripped of pride, and when she did speak, her voice rose and fell as if she were being sorry and righteous to a child.

"Mary Margaret, you've got no right to talk to me like this. You've got no right."

"What are your rights over me?"

Against the hanging top light, Mary Lee's face was in the shadow, but Abraham could see that she was no longer stiff, but bowing her head so that her hair made a thin grey halo.

"I've got the right to have my daughter married to a responsible man, haven't I, so I can be proud of you?" Her lip trembled gently, not in anger. "You've got no right to worry me to a frazzle like this."

Mary Margaret watched the change in her as coolly as if she were analysing the movements of an animal, and as coolly told her, "Look, Mother, all that talk's no good now. I've heard it too often. Now I'm going away. This time I'm really going."

Mary Lee's head shot up again. "You're nothing but an adulteress!"

"Let him without malice cast the first stone."

"I've always done the best I could for you!" Mary Lee's voice went up into a fine scream.

She had finally destroyed Mary Margaret's coolness, and her anger overwhelmed her and she began to shout, close to Mary Lee, backing her towards the table.

"Look, Mother, get this right." She choked, and tried again to speak. "You haven't! You've never loved me and that's all a mother can do! Not eat a child, or mould a child, or guide a child or blackmail a child. Just love it! Suckle it! Love it!"

Mary Lee sank into a chair, explaining, misunderstanding. "I couldn't feed you. I couldn't. I dried up. I couldn't help drying up! Could I? Could I?" She tried to force Mary Margaret to answer and when she wouldn't, she said, "You look like you hate me. Your own mother."

Mary Margaret had found her version of truth a pleasure. She went on, her face pink with excitement under the bright light.

"I hate all of you because you're professional land-poor, deed-grabbing southerners! I hate Julik because he's a professional down-trodden Jew."

As she watched them in the brash light, picking them out, one by one, her voice caught and calmed and seemed to withdraw from them.

"I'm not going to be walked all over. Listen! I thought

I was safe by now. I thought you couldn't do this to me. In one day you can shake me to pieces. I'm going because I'm too damn scared to stay here any longer. Poor old grandmaw. You got her, didn't you? Fed on her and used her to patch your nest. Look at youall!" She walked round the table, studying them each in turn. She stopped in front of Cinny.

"Little A'nt Cinnybug! Cute little thing! Just like a steel wire with a purpose."

She turned her back on her and caught Amelia's eye. "Poor old Amelia! Look at you! Using your memories as rent for a room and board.

"And you!" She was talking quickly now, almost running round the table. "Mary Lee the Right! Armed with disapproval enough to poison the intentions of a saint. And Julik! Julik the Great! Blackmailing his way through life with poverty and talent and a million dead relations."

She stopped, out of breath, watching them, but none of them had an answer. They sat, slapped down like fallen sandbag dummies. It was the look of them that made her decide, quietly again. "You may hate him and he may hate you, but Jew, Gentile and my Aunt Fanny, you're as alike as peas in a pod."

Amelia began to giggle. "Well, are you finished blowing your whistle, little Miss Mouse?" she asked and went on giggling, near to tears.

Mary Lee whispered bitterly to herself, "My own daughter. My own flesh and blood. Pushed away her dessert without touching it. Took it all for granted. Never picked up after herself. Took it for granted. Didn't 'preciate a thing done for her." She raised her head and howled at Mary Margaret for the last time. "You ungrateful little bitch. After all I've done for you!"

The Kiss of Kin

Mary Margaret was swinging towards the dining-room door when the shout caught her. She turned at the door. "Only the first birth is through the mother. The second is through the front door," she said, pleased with herself. She leaned against the door behind her, pushing it open. "Abraham, I'm going to get my bag, I've had enough of this, and if you've got any sense you'll come with me."

He came after her. "I'm not finished here."

"No, you're not, are you? O.K. You keep on. Wade in deeper. Up to your neck." She grinned at him, "What good do you think it will do?" She hadn't exactly called him a fool, but she had so looked it at him that he felt hot, remembering his anger.

He said nothing for a minute, and when he turned back to them, all sitting there waiting, he spoke only the end of his thought. "It's not mine. None of my business." Nobody understood what he meant, and when he went on, "My mother needed you. Sometimes I think it kept her going. But now that I've seen you . . ." he shrugged his shoulders in a little gesture that put them in mind of his mother.

He said to Mary Margaret, touching her, "Let's go."

"Good-bye, Passmores," he called out to them, but still no one moved. "Good-bye, Passmore Place!"

"Cousin Cad," he roused him by name, made him sit up from where he'd slumped down, too dejected to listen any more.

"You want me, son?"

"Cousin Cad, you can take my third of hell, and divide it up, exactly equally, between the resident devils!"

Cadwallader stood up and began to grope for the will again, by habit. "Do you really mean that, Abraham? It's quite a valuable piece of property. Your . . ."

Abraham stopped him. "No. I've found out what I

want to. That's all I want. It's my piece of property."

Cadwallader managed to grin. "Well, that's all fine, son, but you can't borry money on that!" He laughed feebly.

Abraham took Mary Margaret's arm, and then remembered A'nt Elemere. "Good-bye, A'nt Elemere," he called over his shoulder. "Thank you for all that good coffee."

"Wait a minute."

They both stopped at the sound of A'nt Elemere's voice. "Come here to me, Miss Mary Margaret. You too, Mr. Abraham." She stood stock still and waited until they were standing in front of her, side by side, before she bothered to speak again.

"I ainta gonna let you youngins ramp off without finishin' what I got to do. It ain't fair on the Passmores, and it ain't fair on youall."

She hesitated to collect herself. "Now, don't go," she murmured, "I got a lot to say and I got to get it all clear. I'm getting old . . .

"Now I been listenin' to a lot of fine talk from you two young brats, and I ainta gonna have you talkin' that way. Walk out of here in scorn jest as bad as walkin' out of here in hatred. I ainta gonna have it. All this big talk . . . all this fancy laying down the law . . ."

She had found her stride and she went on, more strongly, her voice rising, "Ainta gonna have it. You know a mighty fine lot but you don't know about what nobody else might of been through. You don't know what Miss Cinny was like when she was a youngin, or Miss Amelia."

She brushed past both of them and went to the table where Cinnybug sat with her head down.

"Why, Miss Cinny was as pert and sassy as you could find

anywhere, all full of life, always talking about how she was gonna up and take the steamboat one day all the way to Cincinnati. That's how she come by that nickname, because she had such a bug to get to Cincinnati."

A'nt Elemere looked over Cinny's head at Jellicoe, slouched beside her.

"Well, she musta had. She married for it."

She shouted to Abraham across the room.

"Do you think a girl like she was would have hurt your maw ifn she'd knowed what she was at? Why, she didn't have sense enough to know." Her voice softened again. "You don't expect no little kitten to have horse sense, do you? Well, don't go waiting for it in Miss Cinnybug."

She caught the glint of Amelia's hair as she turned her head in her arms.

"And Miss Amelia. Prettiest youngin I believe I ever did see. Lord's love, you should have seen her ride. You would of thought anybody could ride like that wouldn't of been skeered of nothin'." She reached down and began to stroke her hair. "But she started out being skeered the very day she was married. Most gals does. But Miss Meely never got over it. She never had no chance. Never to know how you're gonna keep body and soul together. . . . Ain't none of youall knows about that marriage, and I ainta gonna tell you." Amelia turned her head a little and sighed in her half-sleep. "She knows. Miss Meely knows. Don't you, honey?"

A'nt Elemere straightened up and looked straight across the table into Mary Lee's eyes.

"As for Miss Mary Lee, I ainta gonna say nothing about her. I never knowed her 'fore she turned ornery . . ."

Mary Margaret tried to stop her by saying, "A'nt Elemere, we didn't mean to. . ."

But she got no further. "That's the trouble!" A'nt

Elemere looked up at her and trounced back across the room. "Don't nobody mean nothing when it's over. Let me tell you somethin', Miss High and Mighty, jest you try spendin' your life bein' bored and disappointed because you jest ain't got gumption enough to do somethin' about it! I seen people sicken and die of jest plain havin' no gumption."

She was very close to Mary Margaret. "I didn't reckon you had enough gumption to slap your mammy down and priss off, but I was wrong. Don't you start laying down the law, jest start thanking the Lord for your luck. Shamey on you! I thought you knowed better!"

"You know I'm ashamed."

"You downright ought to be. Seem like when the Bible say charity begin at home, well seem like to me so does pity."

She turned to the sink, trying to find something to do, because she suddenly realised how much she'd had to say; but still she went on, now softly, almost to herself.

"You learn on your own home-folks what gits on your nerves fore you start out practisin' on the rest of the world." She turned to them again, as if she were surprised that they were still standing there, watching her. "That's all I got to say to you youngins. Git on outa my kitchen. You're the two I ainta gonna worry about!"

"Lord knows why!" Mary Lee muttered, but nobody heard her.

Her voice only made Mary Margaret conscious of her, sitting there, and she was surprised somehow that Mary Lee had frozen back into her old straight-backed way already, as if she had only a memory of being alive since her last high words. She sat there with her hands twined together, straight out in front of her on the table under the bright white bulb.

"Mother."

Mary Lee neither answered nor moved.

"Mother." Mary Margaret bent down over her shoulder and kissed her cold thin cheek.

"Good-bye, Mother." She realised that, for the first time since she could remember, Mary Lee didn't draw back when she was kissed.

"Mother," Mary Margaret whispered again, and hugged her, mussing her hair. Mary Lee never said a word.

As Abraham held open the door for her, Cadwallader called out, "Abraham, don't you want to sign over the rights to your third?"

Abraham looked over his shoulder, "You don't need it, Cad," he called. "You've got three witnesses—twenty-five years of witnesses stuck to this fly-paper."

He shut the door behind him, and even as he started down the dining-room to the hall, he already had trouble remembering what they looked like, except that they were like bundles under the light.

Their footsteps echoed back from the wide, night-lit hall of the Passmore Place, and there was only the dining-room door where they had been, swinging behind them.

Cinnybug's bright voice splintered the silence of the kitchen they had left.

"Does he mean it? Does he really mean it? He must be outa his mind! It's a valuable piece of property!" She looked, pleading for reassurance at Cadwallader.

"We'll be all right now, won't we, Cousin Cad?"

But Cousin Cad had had enough of them. Mechanically, very carefully, he was putting the will back into his brief-case. He locked it and put the key away in his watch pocket before he answered Cinnybug.

"Don't worry about it now, Cinny. I'm pretty tired. I don't want any more fuss," he begged her.

Then, as he picked up the case, he relented a little. After all, it was his job to get things settled, once and for all, if things ever were settled that way.

"If you want me to, I'll drive to see Mr. Crasscopper in the morning and tell him you can pay off three thousand dollars right away. I'm sure Amelia'll see her way clear to helping you raise the rest."

Amelia raised her head out of her arms when she heard her name, and Cinny ran round the table to her. But Amelia didn't notice her at all, only when she said, "Will you, Amelia? Will you do that?"

Amelia was staring straight across the table at Mary Lee, just as A'nt Elemere had done, in judgment.

"Mary Lee, tomorrow you go."

Mary Lee patted her hair where Mary Margaret had mussed it, and pushed herself up from the table by her arms. She gave a long sigh, a yawn, and went to the dining-room door. "Oh, we'll see about that when the time comes, Amelia," she dismissed her. "I've got too much on my mind right now. I'm going to bed."

She was gone before Amelia could answer. She looked round at all of them left and complained, "I'll never get rid of her. Never will. That damn woman'll bury me from here." She put her head back down in her arms, still saying aloud, "Reckon I'd miss her anyway. She belongs here, same as the rest of the junk."

Cinny touched her shoulder to make her look up again. When she didn't, she shook it slightly.

"Amelia, you will let me have your half of the early 'mercan sideboard, won't you? I'll trade you my half of almost anything else!"

Amelia shook her hand away.

"Aw, for God's sake, let me alone."

Cinny kept on at her, begging for an answer.

The Kiss of Kin

"Please, Amelia, aw, please, honey . . ."

But Jellicoe, like Cadwallader, had had about enough of them for one evening, and he began to guide Cinnybug towards the back screen-door, coaxing her, "Come on home, honey, I got to go to work tomorrow."

Cinnybug looked longingly round the room for somebody to ease her mind. She asked A'nt Elemere, "Do you think she will?"

A'nt Elemere came round to her and began to coax, too. "Sure she will, sure Miss Meely will. Don't you worry. You git some sleep."

They had bundled Cinnybug to the door when she broke away from them and turned back, but only to say, as bright as a button for the first time since the evening had begun, "Good-night, Amelia, I'll be back up in the morning!"

From Amelia's arms where her head was cupped came a muffled, "I'll bet you will."

But Cinnybug and Jellicoe had disappeared and they walked down the back path, leaving a trail of fast conversation behind them.

Away from them, in the empty hall, Mary Lee stopped, rigid, forgetting for a second why she'd come out. Then she remembered that she was on her way to bed, the same as she had every night, as if nothing had happened. She dragged herself up the stairs slowly, tireder than she could ever remember being, but when she turned down the hall to her own room she forgot again and went past it, pulling herself on up the attic stairs, into the dark.

There, on the top step, the headache finally focused on her like a giant current, twisting even the darkness into a tighter thing around her, and she began to pace blindly back and forth across the attic floor.

The Kiss of Kin

In the kitchen Cadwallader stopped by Amelia and patted her shoulder.

"Good-bye, Amelia. It's been a sad day. Yes. Glad it's over."

He went out of the back screen-door and A'nt Elemere followed and watched after him, by habit, leaning worn-out against the door-jamb, breathing the night air in long tired sighs. She saw the shadows of Jellicoe and Cinnybug waiting at the gate, but Cadwallader passed them by, his voice floating faintly back, "Good-bye, Cinny, honey, don't you worry. Good-bye, Jellicoe."

Jellicoe's voice carried clear to her in answer in the still late air, "Good-bye, Cad. Come on, Cinny. Golly these things always take so long. Youall can talk the hind-leg off a mule when you get to discussing property."

She heard the car doors slam, and a long beam of light shot on; a motor started and the light came round in a circle, finding the porch, finding A'nt Elemere for a second, then was gone, leaving the darkness darker behind it.

The other car had not started when she came back into the kitchen. Behind her she could hear the kick and choke of a laboured engine. She went up to Amelia, still lying with her head in her arms in the now empty room, barren of any sound or movement.

"Miss Amelia, ain't you ready to go to bed?" There was no answer. She said again, "Miss Meely."

Amelia lifted her head.

"Look in the bread-box, A'nt Elemere; you and me need a drink."

A'nt Elemere got the bottle, and two glasses, and put them on the table as carefully as if she were setting it for a meal.

"Thank you, Miss Amelia," she told her, formally. "I

reckon I would like one to help me sleep." She waited beside the table.

Amelia laughed, a single snort. "That's a fine reason. We'll both have one . . . to help us sleep. Sit down."

A'nt Elemere had been waiting to be asked and now she sat down, as sedate as a tea party, and clasped the glass Amelia handed her in both hands, saying in a nice, strange, conversational voice, "I thought you was keeping it in the flour-bin today." She lifted the drink. "Thank you, Miss Amelia."

They both drank, and set down empty glasses.

"Miss Mary Lee got to find out."

Across the creek, the lights of the last car flashed on, lighting the trees for a minute until the car disappeared down the creek road. Neither of the women in the kitchen saw it; only Mary Lee, who had sunk to the low sill and was trying to cool her head against the glass pane of the attic window, saw, and knew which car it was.

But the car lights and the fireflies and the thing that had happened were all the same to her, nuisance. She asked one question against the window.

"Where in the name of God did I put my luminal?" and left her breath on the glass.

Then, as if the sound of her own voice in the dark, empty attic released her caged thoughts, she began to mutter, got up from the sill, and began to pace back and forth again in the soft darkness.

"What in God's name would they do without me? It's all very well . . ." she stumbled at the bed edge and knocked her shin on one of the brass knobs, making her call out in anger and quick pain, "Has a goddamn one of them ever even bothered to find out how many sheets there are in the house, or where the rugs are so worn out I've got to push the chairs over them every blessed time I go by? Do they think I like it . . ." She went on pacing the floor silently until she had returned to the window. She raised her small veined fist deliberately and drove it into the wooden window-frame, crying out:

"This is all the thanks I get, this is the thanks. . . . What do any of you know, goddamned trifling fools? What did any of you ever bother to learn about me? The whole damn lot of you—pigs in a pen!"

She turned away into the dark again, as if the Passmores were clustered outside the attic window, watching and listening, and she had decided to ignore the whole damn lot, saying to herself:

"They've no idea how lonesome a smart woman can get," then laughed a single, bitter laugh.

"When could they of spared me? When wouldn't they of let the whole damn place go to rack and ruin?"

Then she remembered the car that she had watched disappear down the road. "You think you're so damned smart!" she craned out of the window, stooped, and called to the road where the car had been in her frenzy. "Do you think I wanted you? Hanging around my neck when I was no more than nineteen years old?

"Jesus God, you little hussy, you don't know a damn thing about what somebody else might of been through!"

Nobody heard her but John Junior in the room below, who only woke and turned, not taking in the words, and went to sleep again.

"They haven't a notion," she said, drawing her head in again, calmer, finding the cool pane with her forehead. "Now, what in the world would they do if I just picked up and waltzed off?"

Then, as a last cry, almost not heard, into the room, "Where in the name of God would I go now?"

Like a stab of lightning the headache found and thrust

at the base of her skull, bringing a tidal wave of nausea. Mary Lee sank on to the attic bed among the piles of Miss Anna Mary's papers, her body dead quiet, but her head turning back and forth in the darkness like a hunter.

Only the wet mask of her forehead stayed for a little while on the attic window-pane.

Down below in the kitchen, A'nt Elemere was quiet for a while, sinking into her tiredness, but was roused by the crash of glass on the floor as Amelia pitched forward on to the table and lay still.

A'nt Elemere jumped up and shook her shoulders.

"Miss Amelia! Miss Meely! Wake up, Miss Meely!"

But she knew it was no use. She sighed, "Oh, well, it ain't the first time I put that youngin to bed."

Then, suddenly, it was all too much for her. She started to moan, and through the moaning stumbled snatches of her deep hurt, aloud in the still kitchen, ". . . all these youngins . . ." Her face screwed up, "Here you done went and forgot about me altogether . . ."

. . . .

Abraham drove on down the now familiar creek road, which seven hours before had been so strange, intent on the tunnel of light ahead of him down the black road. What he thought were sobs came from Mary Margaret, lying where John Junior had lain, in the front seat beside him.

It wasn't until the main road that he realised she was giggling. He was furious, fooled. "For God's sake!"

It only made her giggle more, huddled, trying to stop.

"What's so funny?"

She stopped long enough to tell him, "I've got to go to the depot. It's no use . . ."

He drove on, silently, into his own headlight; the

road, the house, the whole thing dwindling and disappearing in the dark behind him; only the stranger cousin from it, like flotsam, left on the car seat.

"I've still got Julik's railroad ticket," she explained, and went on laughing.

MARY LEE SETTLE grew up in West Virginia and attended Sweetbriar College, which she left in the early years of World War II to enlist in the British Royal Air Force. Her war experiences formed the background for a memoir titled *All the Brave Promises*. After the war she stayed in England and masqueraded for a year as Mrs. Charles Palmer, "etiquette expert" for *Woman's Day*. Since that time she has traveled the world, always bringing far corners deeply into her novels. She is the author of *The Love Eaters, The Clam Shell, The Beulah Quintet*, and a new novel, *Celebration*. In 1978, *Blood Tie* won the National Book Award for Fiction.